BEAGLE in a BACKPACK

Ben M. Baglio

Illustrations by Ann Baum

Cover illustration by
Mary Ann Lasher

AN
APPLE
PAPERBACK

SCHOLASTIC INC.
New York Toronto London Auckland Sydney
Mexico City New Delhi Hong Kong Buenos Aires

Special thanks to Andrea Abbott

No part of this publication may be reproduced or stored in a retrieval system, or transmitted in any form or by any means, electronic, mechanical, photocopying, recording, or otherwise, without written permission of the publisher. For information regarding permission, write to Working Partners Limited, 1 Albion Place, London W6 0QT, United Kingdom.

ISBN 0-439-77521-3

12 11 10 9 8 7 6 5 4   6 7 8 9 10/0

Printed in the U.S.A.   40
First Scholastic printing, September 2005

One

"Bobby! No!"

The cry stopped Mandy Hope in her tracks and she whirled around.

A black-and-white kitten had escaped from his basket on the other side of the waiting room. His owner, a young woman with a baby in one arm, lunged forward to catch him with the other, but the kitten was too quick for her. He darted across the room with his tail stuck straight out behind him.

Mandy dropped the X-rays she'd been taking to her mom and hurried over. Kneeling down, she put out her hand. "Come here, Bobby," she murmured.

The black-and-white kitten scrunched himself up against the wall and hissed.

"I won't hurt you," Mandy promised, stretching her hand out farther. But before she could touch him, he shot past her and hurtled toward the reception desk. His tail was so fluffed out that it looked like a black bottle-brush.

The kitten jumped onto the desk, startling Jean Knox, the Animal Ark receptionist. He then tried to leap over a nearby filing cabinet, but he misjudged the height and landed short.

"Bobby!" His owner gasped as the bristling little creature tumbled toward the ground. Cleverly twisting in midair, he landed on his paws in true feline style and rushed straight for the glass door that led out of the waiting room. A man carrying a budgie in a cage was just about to open it.

"Wait!" Mandy yelled, reaching the door in three giant strides and scooping Bobby up just as the man came in.

He looked at Mandy and the kitten and raised his eyebrows. "Busy today?"

"Not really," Mandy said breathlessly. "Just a normal Saturday morning at Animal Ark!" She grinned at him over her shoulder as she returned Bobby to his grateful owner before picking up the X-rays to take to her mom.

Mandy's mom and dad were both vets. They ran a busy clinic called Animal Ark that was attached to their home in Welford, a village in the English county of Yorkshire. For as long as she could remember, twelve-year-old Mandy had helped out in the clinic. On top of her regular duties—cleaning out cages and feeding the animals in the residential unit—she was also quick to respond in emergencies, such as escaping kittens!

Dr. Emily was examining an old springer spaniel who had started limping a couple of days before. Simon, Animal Ark's veterinary nurse, was holding the dog still while the spaniel's owner watched anxiously.

Dr. Emily glanced across at Mandy. "Everything all right in there?"

"Fine," Mandy told her. "Just a kitten getting a bit spooked."

"Well, it *is* nearly Halloween," joked Simon.

Mandy laughed. "And he *is* a black kitten! He sure scared Jean when he landed on her desk!"

There was a knock at the door then, followed by James's voice. "Are you in there, Mandy?"

"Coming," Mandy called.

"He sounds eager to find you," said Dr. Emily. She held one of the X-rays up to the light and studied it.

"Probably because he has some sick practical joke to play on me." Mandy grinned. She opened the door cautiously, half expecting to come face-to-face with a ghoulish mask.

There was no apparition waiting for her on the other side, just James grinning from ear to ear. He was holding his hands carefully behind his back. "Hi, Mandy," he said, his eyes glinting behind his glasses. "You'll never guess what I've got."

Mandy imagined something like a squirt gun that shot out slimy green goo, or a plastic spider. She hoped it wasn't anything too scary that might frighten the animals in the waiting room and cause a repeat performance of Bobby's dash for freedom. She glanced at the kitten and saw that he was still curled up safely inside his carrying case. His owner had put a stack of heavy magazines on the lid to stop him from pushing it open again.

"Is it a trick?" she asked.

"Nope. But it *is* something really cool," James said, beaming. "Or should I say, something really *jolly* and *merry*!"

"Jolly and merry? That sounds Christmasy," said Mandy. "You're kind of early. It's only October." She spotted the corner of a box sticking out from behind James's back. "Hang on! I know what 'jolly and merry' means!"

With a flourish, James produced a huge silver box tied with orange ribbon. "Jolly Jims from Merry's!" he announced. "They sent them as a Halloween present."

During a trip to York, the two friends had gone on a tour of Merry's chocolate factory. While they were there, James had invented some candies that he named *Jolly Jims.*

"Not just Jolly Jims," he went on, taking off the lid to reveal a tempting assortment of treats. "There's just about every type of chocolate here."

"That's fantastic!" Mandy exclaimed. "It should last you at least — let me see . . ." She tapped her cheek with one finger as if she were doing a difficult math problem. "At least three days of the midterm vacation."

James grinned. "Make that a day and a half, since you'll be sharing them. We're going to use them as brain food while we figure out our trick-or-treat plans for Friday night."

"Good idea," Mandy said enthusiastically. "When do we start?"

"How about now?" James suggested.

Mandy looked doubtfully at the patients who were waiting to see her mom and dad. "I'm not sure," she began.

A loud squawk interrupted her as a tall, balding man and a dark-haired little girl came into the waiting room. The man was almost hidden behind a large birdcage, but Mandy recognized him at once. Mr. Parker Smythe was a very wealthy man who worked in satellite television, and the little girl was his seven-year-old daughter, Imogen.

As Mandy went over to say hello, she couldn't take her eyes off the magnificent bird sitting on a perch in the cage. It looked to be a little under three feet high, and it was the most beautiful color imaginable — a deep cobalt blue, with wide, sunshine yellow rings surrounding its eyes. Its curved black bill was huge and sharply pointed.

"What a bird!" Mandy gasped.

"Yeah. That's a beautiful parrot!" agreed James.

"It's a macaw," Imogen informed James.

"I've never seen a macaw that color," Mandy said, thinking of the bright red and gold birds her parents had treated. "It must be a very special one."

Mr. Parker Smythe carefully put the cage down on the reception desk. "You're right. She is very special," he said. "She's a hyacinth macaw, one of the rarest macaws in the world. Worth a fortune, too."

Jean raised her eyebrows, then peered more closely at the bird. "She's exquisite all right." She took a card out from a drawer and picked up a pen. "Name?"

"Ronald Parker Smythe."

"No, I mean the bird's name," Jean corrected him with a smile.

"Oh, right," said Mr. Parker Smythe. "Portia." He

stroked the macaw's head through the top of the cage. "Is there a long wait?" he asked.

"Not too long," she replied. "Take a seat and we'll call you."

Mr. Parker Smythe glanced around the room. "I think I'll stand," he said. "Do you mind if I open the window?"

Jean looked surprised. "Well, I don't know," she said hesitantly. "It's pretty cold outside."

"Well, I'm concerned about Portia catching germs," argued Mr. Parker Smythe.

"What's the matter with her?" Mandy asked, going over to the window with Mr. Parker Smythe and opening it a crack. She hoped her parents would be able to see Portia before the waiting room got too drafty.

"I'm not sure," he said. "She's just not as alert as she was when she first came to us. And she's regurgitated her food a couple of times, which can't be healthy."

The door to Dr. Emily's examining room opened and Simon came out with the spaniel and his owner, who was looking a lot happier than before. Whatever was causing the limp couldn't be too serious.

Simon called in the next patient. Mandy was glad to see it was Bobby the kitten. The sooner he was on his way home, the better!

Imogen was still standing beside James, looking rather bored.

"Aren't you lucky to have such a beautiful bird?" Mandy said to her.

Imogen shrugged. "I guess. But she's not as cute as my bunnies." Mandy knew Imogen had four rabbits that she shared with eleven-year-old John Hardy, who lived at the Fox and Goose Inn with his dad and stepmother. Imogen had the rabbits when John was away at boarding school, and he looked after them during vacations. "You can't cuddle a macaw like you can cuddle bunnies," Imogen added.

"I guess not," Mandy said. "But that's not the only reason to like pets."

"My mom likes Portia because she matches the new wallpaper in the dining room," Imogen said calmly.

Mandy was taken aback. "Er, that's not really what I meant," she said.

Catching Mandy's eye and looking equally stunned, James took the lid off the box of chocolates and offered them to Imogen. "Does Portia talk?" he asked Mr. Parker Smythe.

"Not much. But she's good at imitating sounds," answered Mr. Parker Smythe. "Or rather, *was* good. Lately, she's hardly made a sound, aside from the occasional squawk."

As if to confirm this, Portia fluffed out her feathers,

then shuffled to the end of her perch and sat hunched up against the cage looking sorry for herself.

Mandy would have liked to pet her but knew better than to put her hand into the cage. Portia's beak was capable of giving someone a nasty peck, and if she was feeling sick, she probably wouldn't want a stranger touching her. Instead Mandy said softly, "Don't worry, Portia. You've come to the right place. Mom and Dad will find out what's wrong, and soon you'll be as bright as a button again."

"She'll never be as bright as Button," said Imogen. Button was the name of one of her bunnies. Imogen unwrapped a foil-covered chocolate and popped it into her mouth.

"I don't think Mandy was talking about *your* Button," said Mr. Parker Smythe. He looked up as Mandy's dad appeared at the door of his examining room.

"Who's next?" Dr. Adam asked Jean.

Jean looked at her appointment book. "Let's see. The budgie and the rabbit are waiting for Dr. Emily. And Portia's for you." She pointed to the macaw.

Dr. Adam looked appreciatively at the magnificent bird and said, "Come in, Ronald. And Mandy and James, I might need a hand, so you'd better come in, too."

They went into the room, and Mr. Parker Smythe

described Portia's symptoms. "She's pretty miserable," he began, putting the cage on the stainless steel examination table. "Lethargic, even. Not nearly as active as when she first arrived."

"Where did you get her?" asked Dr. Adam.

"She was a gift from a colleague," said Mr. Parker Smythe. "It'll be very embarrassing if he comes over and sees her in this state. Or worse, if she dies and he finds out."

"Dies?" Dr. Adam frowned at Mr. Parker Smythe. "Who said anything about her dying?"

"No one," answered Mr. Parker Smythe. "But being an exotic bird, she's bound to be susceptible to all sorts of things. You know, diseases that she wouldn't encounter in her natural habitat. Even the climate inside our house could upset her. That's why I've been trying to do everything by the book." He sighed and shook his head. "It doesn't seem to have helped, though."

"I don't think you should blame yourself," said Dr. Adam. "We don't know what's wrong with her yet."

Portia was pecking halfheartedly at some seeds in a feed tray attached to the side of the cage. Suddenly, she spit them up again, then settled back on her perch, looking thoroughly exhausted. Mandy's heart went out to her.

"Does she do that often?" asked Dr. Adam.

"Several times since yesterday," Mr. Parker Smythe admitted.

The regurgitated seeds had landed in the water trough.

"I'll get some fresh water," James offered as Mandy's dad opened the cage and removed the plastic container. "Thanks, James," he said, handing it to him. "Mandy, please get a towel so we can take Portia out."

Mandy took a clean towel out of a cupboard and gave it to her dad. Portia craned her neck and tried to bite Dr. Adam, but he quickly wrapped the towel around her, trapping her wings close to her sides, and eased her out of the cage. He tucked her securely under one arm and grasped her head between his thumb and fingers. "There," he said. "Now I can have a good look at you."

Portia stared straight ahead while Dr. Adam felt her keel—the ridge on her breastbone. After a while she started wriggling her wings, so he put her on the table. "Hold her head, please, Mandy, and James, you hold her body."

"The keel's protruding," he said after feeling it again. "Which means she's lost weight. When did you notice her change, Ronald?"

"A couple of days ago," answered Mr. Parker Smythe.

Dr. Adam sucked in his breath. "That could mean she's pretty sick," he said quietly.

Mandy's stomach flipped over. Her dad wouldn't say something like that unless an animal was in pretty bad shape. "How do you know?" she asked. Aside from seeming a bit miserable and having lost some weight, Portia didn't look too bad.

"Well, because birds are preyed upon by lots of animals in the food chain, they don't generally show signs of being sick until the illness is at fairly advanced stage," Dr. Adam explained.

"Do you mean she *is* dying?" asked Mr. Parker Smythe in dismay.

"All I'm saying is that Portia's probably a lot sicker than she appears," responded Dr. Adam. "I'll need to take blood and do some tests, and perhaps even take some X-rays."

With Mandy and James still holding Portia, Dr. Adam gently inserted a damp ear plug into her throat, then quickly removed it and wiped the smear onto a glass slide. He peered at it through the microscope. "I can't see anything out of the ordinary there." Next he parted the feathers on Portia's neck and drew a small amount of blood. She struggled a bit, but Mandy and James kept a firm grip on her.

"I'll send this sample away for full bloodwork," said

Dr. Adam. "In the meantime, we'll keep her in the residential unit so that I can observe her."

"The residential unit!" Mr. Parker Smythe sounded very unhappy. "But she could pick up germs from the other animals!"

"Well, we could keep her in the wildlife unit. It's empty right now so there's no chance she'll catch anything in there," said Dr. Adam.

Mandy and James carefully returned the macaw to her cage. Portia shook herself, then fluffed up her feathers and sat hunched on the floor of the cage, her head drooping.

"Poor girl," Mandy murmured.

The phone rang. Portia blinked and put her head on one side. Dr. Adam picked up the receiver.

"Adam Hope," he began, then looked rather surprised when the ringing continued. "What on earth?" he said while the puzzled voice on the other end of the line asked, "Hello? Hello? Is anyone there?"

"It's all right, Dad," smiled Mandy. "It's only Portia playing a Halloween trick on you!" She could see that Portia had opened her beak a tiny bit to imitate the ringing noise. It was a heartwarming sign.

If Portia still had her sense of humor, surely her illness couldn't be *that* serious.

Two

"I think you should work for Merry's full time, James," said Mandy, licking chocolate off her fingers. "Jolly Jims are delicious."

"They *are* pretty good," James agreed. He helped himself to another one and passed the box to Dr. Adam.

After settling Portia in the wildlife unit, Mandy and James had joined Dr. Adam and Dr. Emily, Jean, and Simon in the kitchen for a snack.

Mandy's dad snuck a glance at Dr. Emily, who was paging through a veterinary journal, then helped himself to several Jolly Jims.

"I saw that, Adam," said Dr. Emily, not lifting her eyes. "One's enough!"

"Women!" Dr. Adam sighed, putting all but one of the pieces of candy back in the box before passing it to Simon. "They've got eyes in the top of their head."

Jean put a fresh pot of tea and a pitcher of juice on the table and picked up the newspaper. "Oh, my," she said. "Look at this." She turned the paper so that everyone could see the main headline. FOURTEEN-YEAR-OLD GIRL MISSING, it read.

"Who is it?" Mandy asked. It could be someone she knew, even someone who went to school in Walton with her and James.

Jean scanned the article. "Amber Hutton," she said. "Do you know her?"

Mandy shook her head.

Jean began to read aloud. *"Fourteen-year-old Amber Hutton has disappeared from her home in Walton. Police believe she may have run away. Her anxious parents are baffled by her absence. She's quiet and somewhat shy, but as far as they know, she's not being bullied at school or having any trouble with her studies."*

Jean read aloud more of the article. Amber, far from being unhappy, had been thrilled recently after getting a part-time job at the local dog-rescue center. She loved dogs and had her heart set on working with them when she finished school.

"Sounds like a girl after your own heart, Mandy," remarked Jean.

"Except I don't think I'd ever run away," Mandy said.

"Maybe Amber hasn't run away," suggested James. "She could have been kidnapped."

"I hope you're wrong about that," said Dr. Emily. "Her poor parents must be out of their minds with worry. Oh, no," she said then, glancing out of the window. "We've lost track of time. Walter is arriving for his appointment."

Walter Pickard, a retired butcher, was bringing his three cats, Missie, Tom, and Flicker, for their annual checkup. Dr. Emily hurried out of the kitchen, pulling on her white coat.

For the rest of the day, Animal Ark was busier than ever, so it wasn't until that evening that Mandy and James got a chance to start planning their trick-or-treating.

"I brought a map of Welford," said James, unfolding it on the Hopes' living room floor. "We could start up here," he suggested, pointing, "and stop at Beacon House first." That was where the Parker Smythe family lived.

Mandy wasn't sure this was a good idea. "They probably won't be in the mood for tricks or treats if Portia's still ill. I think we'd better skip them this year."

"How about starting here, then?" James stabbed his forefinger at the other end of the village, where Mandy's grandparents lived.

Dr. Emily suddenly leaned forward to pick up the TV remote control and raise the volume. "Hang on a minute, you two," she said. "They're talking about the missing girl."

"Our main story this evening concerns missing schoolgirl Amber Hutton," the announcer was saying as his voice became audible.

"Maybe they've found her?" Mandy said, her heart lifting.

"There has been no sign of Amber since she disappeared late Thursday afternoon." The announcer dashed Mandy's hopes. *"But in an unexpected twist, it appears that she may not be alone."*

"See! She *has* been kidnapped," concluded James.

"Shhh!" Mandy hissed.

"According to Linda Davis, the owner of Little Briar Dog Rescue Center, where Amber worked," continued the announcer, *"a ten-week-old beagle puppy named Frisbee is also missing, along with several packets of food and a blanket."*

"She's run off with the puppy!" Mandy gasped.

"Shhh!" It was James's turn to demand silence.

The anchorman explained that a litter of four beagle puppies had been abandoned at the shelter one week earlier. Amber had volunteered to take care of them and had bonded with them very quickly. *"Ms. Davis said that Amber stopped by every morning on her way to school and then again in the afternoon to look after the dogs,"* reported the anchorman.

Apparently, no one had any idea why Amber would

have run off with Frisbee. Her parents were as confused as everyone else. In an interview, they said that Amber, who was last seen wearing a blue jacket and black jeans, hadn't even hinted that she'd like to keep the puppy. "And why would she have run off with just one of the litter when she was so fond of all four pups?" asked Mrs. Hutton.

"Why, indeed?" agreed Dr. Emily, turning the volume back down as the anchorman went on to the next story.

"Well, four puppies would be a huge handful," James commented. "It must be hard enough coping with one when you're on the run."

"Whatever the reason, it's a really selfish thing to do," Mandy muttered. She imagined the poor little beagle being taken suddenly from its siblings, and carted around from one uncomfortable and unfamiliar place to another. "How on earth does that girl think she's going to take care of a puppy all by herself?"

Dr. Adam was fiddling with a big flashlight. "Aren't you being a bit harsh, honey?" He put the batteries back in the flashlight and screwed on the end. "You're a good two years younger than Amber, and I'd trust you to take care of a puppy any day."

Mandy appreciated her dad's confidence in her. All the same, it would have been impossible to grow up at

Animal Ark and not know how to look after an animal. "Yes, but I've had tons of experience," she reminded her dad.

"And Amber's been working at a dog shelter. She wouldn't have gotten the job if she wasn't up to it," said Dr. Emily. She curled her legs up beneath her on the sofa and picked up her book. "It sounds to me as if she's doing her best to take care of Frisbee. Otherwise she wouldn't have bothered with the blanket and the food, would she?"

"I hope you're right," was all Mandy could say. As far as she was concerned, a ten-week-old puppy needed a lot more than food and a blanket. *A stable and loving home, for starters*, she thought. *And how will he get that with someone who's running away?*

Three

All during the next day, Mandy could think of nothing other than the missing girl and the beagle pup. Even a trip with her grandparents, Tom and Dorothy Hope, to watch a battle reenactment at a local castle couldn't distract her. As the two armies clashed ferociously under a low gray sky, Mandy kept imagining Amber battling to keep out of sight. Then, when it started to rain and the spectators scurried for shelter, Mandy could think only of little Frisbee, damp, cold, and without the comfort of the other puppies, let alone his mother.

"Cheer up, sweetheart," said Mandy's grandma when

they were sitting inside the cozy café that had once been the gatehouse to the castle. She paused while a waitress brought them three mugs of steaming hot chocolate. "Thank you," Gran said. Then she looked at Mandy again and added, "Someone will find Amber and the puppy soon, you'll see."

Outside, driving rain lashed the windows of the café and a strong wind whipped across the moor, making the sheep on a nearby hillside huddle together for warmth. "But they've been missing for two whole days!" Mandy told her grandparents. "And the weather's getting worse."

Tom Hope put an arm around her shoulders. "You worry too much, Mandy. Amber's probably gone to stay with one of her friends."

Mandy thought this was unlikely. Just about everyone in Walton and the surrounding villages must have heard about Amber by now. If she *was* with a friend, their parents would have called Amber's mom and dad. No—wherever Amber and Frisbee were, they were well hidden.

Back at Animal Ark, Mandy called out to her parents as she opened the front door. "Any news of Amber and Frisbee?"

"Nothing yet," Dr. Emily replied from the living room.

"And Portia?" Mandy asked, taking off her jacket in the hall. She crossed her fingers. There had to be *some* good news.

Dr. Adam was coming downstairs. "I'm afraid not," he said. He put an arm around Mandy and they went into the living room together. "She's even more listless than when she arrived, and she's lost more weight."

The double dose of bad news had been a blow to Mandy. She couldn't bring herself to continue with Halloween preparations that evening, so she called James to cancel. "Maybe I'll feel more like it tomorrow," she told him. This was turning into a miserable midterm vacation! Part of Mandy wished she were back at school, while the other part clung to a sliver of hope that the morning would bring better news.

But Monday's paper reported that there was still no sign of Amber, and when Mandy went to check on Portia, she found the bird hunched up at the bottom of her cage with her head drooping and eyes tightly shut.

"Portia," Mandy whispered.

The macaw opened her eyes and looked blankly at Mandy for a moment before closing them again. Mandy went through the motions of giving her fresh water and seeds, wondering all the time if there was any point. If

Portia was losing weight, she was obviously not eating very much.

"She's not looking too good, is she?"

Mandy jumped. She'd been so preoccupied she hadn't heard her dad come in. She frowned. "You still don't have any idea what's wrong with her?"

Dr. Adam shook his head. "I've checked her for parasites, but she's clear. The results of the bloodwork should be back later today or tomorrow morning. Maybe they'll shed some light on things."

"And X-rays?" Mandy asked.

"Done, but those have drawn a blank, too," said her dad.

Portia made a halfhearted attempt to peck at some seeds, but soon gave up.

Mandy couldn't stop thinking about what her dad had said about birds when Mr. Parker Smythe brought Portia in on Saturday. *They don't generally show signs of being sick until the illness is at a fairly advanced stage.* Did this mean that it was too late for Portia? Mandy couldn't bear the thought of this beautiful bird dying because they couldn't figure out what was wrong with her!

"You've *got* to find out!" she urged her dad.

"We're doing our best," he promised, patting her shoulder reassuringly.

*   *   *

Mr. Parker Smythe was just as eager to see his prize bird recover. He arrived at Animal Ark around mid-morning to see how she was.

"She's no better, I'm afraid," Mandy warned him before taking him to the wildlife unit.

Mr. Parker Smythe frowned when he saw Portia. "She's really taken a turn for the worse." He got right to the point when he was called in to see Dr. Adam. "Look here, Adam, I can't possibly lose this bird. If you don't come up with a diagnosis soon, I've got to consult a macaw specialist."

Mandy's initial and silent reaction was that this was probably a very good idea. Someone who treated only macaws might have seen the same symptoms before. *But Mom and Dad are brilliant vets*, she told herself as she took a bottle of disinfectant out of a cupboard. *They'll keep on trying until they find out what is wrong.*

She wiped down the examination table for the next patient, but she couldn't wipe away the nagging worry that by the time a diagnosis was made, it could be too late for Portia.

After lunch, Mandy accompanied her dad on his rounds in the Land Rover. Their first stop was a sheep farm high on the moor three miles outside Welford. The owner, Dora Janecki, had called Animal Ark to say a ewe had caught her foot in a narrow gap between two rocks. The animal had damaged her hoof pulling herself free, so Dora had brought her down from the moor and put her in the barn.

With Dora leading the way, Mandy and her dad entered the windowless stone building that stood alongside the farmhouse. In the gloom, Mandy could just make out the white coat of the ewe. She seemed to be the only sheep in there and she looked anxiously at Dr. Adam, Mandy, and Dora as they approached.

"Don't be afraid," Mandy said, stroking the ewe's head and neck while her dad examined the hoof. It was split almost all the way to the toe.

"I'll have to trim it," said Dr. Adam. "But I'll need more light." He took his flashlight out of his vet's bag. It was the same one he'd been fixing the other evening. "Darn!" he said when he switched it on and no beam appeared. "It's still not working."

"I'll open the big door," said Dora. She was a small, wiry woman with gray hair; if Mandy had been asked to sum her up in one word, she'd have said "sharp," for Dora's chistled features matched her hard voice and her piercing eyes. In all the years that Mandy had known her, she had hardly ever seen Dora smile. But the woman had a good heart and took wonderful care of her large flock of sheep.

Dora swung the big door open. Like the day before, the weather was dismal and wet, so the light that entered the barn made very little difference.

"We'll need that old oil lamp as well," said Dora. She brought it from the far corner of the barn and lit the wick. The pool of light made her look more wizened than ever. *Like a witch*, Mandy couldn't help thinking. *Just in time for Halloween!*

Mandy bent down and picked up the ewe's foreleg, holding the hoof inside the circle of light and high enough for her dad to see it. The ewe looked at her in surprise for a moment, then started to nibble the collar of Mandy's jacket.

"We'll have this taken care of in a flash," said Dr. Adam. He took a hoof-paring knife out of his bag and gently removed the damaged sections of the hoof without inflicting any pain on the ewe.

"There," he said when it was neatly trimmed. "All done."

Mandy patted the ewe on the neck. "I guess you can go back to your herd now."

"I'll take her up to the moor after lunch," said Dora.

Dr. Adam snuffed out the oil lamp. "Could you put this away please, Mandy?"

She carried the lamp back to the darkened corner and balanced it on a bale of hay next to a packet of sandwiches. Mandy guessed they were Dora's lunch. As Dora was leaving the barn with Dr. Adam, Mandy called out to her, "You forgot your sandwiches!"

Dora looked back and waved a hand in Mandy's direction. "Leave them there. Someone's been sleeping in the barn—a tramp, I think!" Her voice softened as she came back over to Mandy. "Poor devil, it can't be fun in this weather. The least I can do is give him a little food."

Mandy was surprised. It was rare for Dora to show sympathy for anyone who wasn't directly helping her sheep. "How do you know someone's sleeping in here?" She couldn't see any belongings or a makeshift bed.

"I heard him last night." Dora said. "The side door slammed shut, and I knew I'd closed it earlier. I thought it was some kids playing a Halloween prank." She shook her head. "Silly holiday," she muttered, and Mandy made a mental note not to include Syke Farm in her trick-or-treat rounds.

"I aimed a flashlight in here but I didn't see anyone," Dora continued. "If it had been kids, I'm sure they'd have tried to scare me. So I guessed it was a vagrant who slipped away when he heard me coming. Then I found his blanket this morning." She picked up a dark gray blanket from a pile of hay nearby.

"You wouldn't think that was enough to keep anyone warm at night," Mandy remarked, touching the coarse fabric. There was a red-and-white label in one corner.

Dora put the blanket down and started back toward the door, where Dr. Adam was waiting. Mandy followed her. "I'll leave an old quilt in here tonight with the food," said Dora quietly.

Mandy wondered how many other people had been lucky enough to catch a glimpse of Dora's soft side.

Dr. Adam tapped his watch. "Come on, Mandy. We still have two more calls to make this morning."

As they drove away, Mandy looked back and waved to Dora. "You know, she's really very kindhearted," she announced. "Who'd have guessed that she'd worry about a tramp's blanket. . . ." She trailed off. *The blanket!* She felt as if she'd missed something very important. But what?

"The label!" she suddenly cried. "Why didn't I notice it before?" She grabbed her dad's arm. "We have to go back to the farm!" she told him. "The label on the blanket said Little Briar! That's got to be the Little Briar Dog Rescue Center!"

Dr. Adam frowned. "So?"

"Little Briar," Mandy said impatiently, "is where Amber worked! It's not a tramp sleeping in Dora's barn. It's Amber and Frisbee!"

Four

As soon as her dad pulled to a halt, Mandy leaped out of the Land Rover and raced over to the farmhouse.

Dora was surprised to see her again so soon. "Did you forget something?" she asked when she opened the door.

"No. I *remembered* something." Mandy quickly filled Dora in on the details about Amber and the missing beagle.

"I heard something about that young girl on TV," said Dora when Mandy had finished.

By then, Dr. Adam had parked. He ran across to join Mandy and Dora on the porch. It was starting to rain, and he had to duck through the drops that fell from the roof like a bead curtain.

"We have to find Amber and Frisbee before the weather gets worse," Mandy said.

"But they might not even be here anymore," reasoned Dr. Adam. "We'd have seen them if they were still in the barn."

"That doesn't mean they're not close by," Mandy pointed out. "There must be tons of places where they could hide." She gestured to all the outbuildings. There were several sheds, another barn, a double garage, and a storeroom. "If we take Tess and Whistler, we'll find them in a flash."

"They're not tracker dogs," Dora reminded Mandy. "They're border collies, bred for herding sheep."

"But they've got good noses! If they pick up Frisbee's scent on the blanket they might be able to track him." In all her dealings with dogs, Mandy had learned never to underestimate what they could do. All dogs could hear or smell something long before a person could.

Dora frowned. "It's worth a try, I suppose." She looked over her shoulder and gave a short, shrill whistle.

Almost immediately, two black-and-white dogs slipped around the half-open door to the farmhouse. They leaped around Dora as if they couldn't wait to go out to work.

"Steady! You're not sheepdogs today," Dora said, her fondness for them coming through in her voice.

Mandy was impatient to start. "Let's go!" she urged.

They ran through the drizzle to the barn, then took the dogs to where the blanket was lying on the hay.

"Here, Tess! Here, Whistler!" Mandy said, pointing to it. She didn't want to touch the blanket in case she confused the dogs with a different scent.

But the border collies showed no interest in the blanket. They sniffed around the hay, then Whistler found an old rat hole and pawed at it eagerly. Mandy's shoulders drooped. So much for her plan to track Amber and Frisbee using the superpowers of dogs! It looked like ordinary human eyesight would have to do.

Dr. Adam came to the same conclusion. "I don't think the dogs understand what we're getting at. It'll be better if we call the police and get them to come up and search."

"But if we hang around waiting for them to show up, we'll lose time," Mandy argued. She peered outside. "The clouds are really low. It's going to pour soon. And it's freezing." Her fingers were numb even though she'd only been outside for a short time.

"I suppose there's no harm in having a quick look around," said Dr. Adam. "But if we don't find them soon"— he looked at Mandy in a way that showed just how well he knew her—"we're not going off on any wild goose chase. We'll get the police to arrange a real search party. Agreed?"

"OK." Mandy knew her dad was probably right. Amber and Frisbee could be far away by now.

While they were talking, Tess had begun to show some interest in the blanket. She sniffed at it and then looked back at Dora and wagged her tail.

"Hang on. We might have a tracker after all," said Dora.

"Good girl, Tess!" Mandy exclaimed, patting the dog. "Where should we start?" she asked Dora.

"We can try the other barn," suggested Dora.

But there was no sign of the missing pair in the small barn. Nor in any of the other buildings. Soon the dogs lost interest and padded behind Dora looking rather bored.

"We should call the police now," said Dr. Adam when they'd searched the last outbuilding. "Amber and Frisbee could be anywhere out there." He waved his arm at the hundreds of acres of empty land. "We could search for a week and not cross paths with them."

Mandy didn't want to give up just yet. "We haven't checked the garage."

"They're not there," said Dora. "I was in there right before you arrived." All the same, she opened the creaking doors and they went inside.

The garage was crammed with all sorts of things ranging from farm implements to old gardening tools. In fact, it seemed to house everything but a car.

Mandy peered into dark corners and behind boxes. An old wardrobe stashed up against the back wall turned out to be empty except for a startled field mouse that scurried out when the mirrored doors were opened.

"What's under here?" Mandy asked, spotting something bulky beneath a tarpaulin. Judging from the shape, it was probably an ancient plow or an old wood-burning stove.

"That's just my—" Dora began as Mandy lifted the edge of the cover.

"Your four-wheeler," Mandy finished for her when she saw the bright green motorbike. Mandy and James had driven it during lambing time in the spring when they'd helped bring the flock down from the high moor. She turned to her dad with a hopeful smile. "This could be just what we need to look for Amber and Frisbee! If they're running across the moor, we'll catch up with them in no time." She appealed to Dora. "What do you think?"

"I think that's a very sensible idea," said Dora, surprising

Mandy. She took a key out of her pocket and gave it to Dr. Adam. "Would you drive it, Doctor? I'm up to my eyeballs with work to do before the day ends."

Dr. Adam took the key. "You're sure you don't mind?"

"I'd say it if I did." Dora sounded more like her usual bad-tempered self. "Now go on, before the weather closes in and that girl gets herself and the pup lost." She folded the bike's cover onto an old chest. "You can ride on back, Mandy. There's a spare helmet on that shelf over there. Two sets of eyes will be better than one."

In the end, it was four sets of eyes that scanned the moor for Amber and Frisbee. Unable to resist joining in, Tess and Whistler sprinted alongside the sturdy four-wheeler while Mandy clung on behind her dad, her arms wrapped tightly around his waist.

She concentrated hard as they zigzagged across the moor, looking for a flash of Amber's blue jacket or a sudden movement.

Once, she saw something disappear behind a low stone wall. "Over there!" she said to her dad, her voice carried away by the wind so that she had to shout. "Behind that wall." But when they got there with the dogs panting at their side, Mandy leaped off the bike to investigate and saw it was just a paper bag.

Disappointed, she climbed back on the bike. The drizzle

soon turned into a downpour and the wind picked up speed, blowing the rain straight into Mandy's eyes until she could hardly see through the visor of her helmet.

Dr. Adam was having the same trouble. "We'll have to go back. I can hardly see where I'm going. And we're drenched."

As much as she wanted to continue, Mandy knew it was impossible. Now it was up to the police. But how much success would they have in this weather? It was raining so hard, it was difficult to see more than a few yards ahead.

They were nearing the farmhouse when Mandy thought she saw something blue sticking out from behind a clump of bushes. Her heart skipped a beat.

"It'll probably be a piece of litter again," Dr. Adam warned. But he slowed down and Mandy jumped off the bike and went to investigate. The blue object turned out to be a ratty-looking shopping bag. Probably an old one of Dora's that had found its way outside, she decided.

"It's nothing. Just another bag," Mandy called to her dad. As she turned to walk away, she slipped on the wet grass and her foot banged into the bag. There was something bulky inside. "Wait," she muttered, reaching into the bag and pulling out a small cardboard packet. "Dog food!" she exclaimed. "Dad, it's *puppy* food. It must be the food that Amber took from Little Briar." Her eyes shone as she ran back to the four-wheeler and showed her dad. "So they *have* been here."

"It seems so," agreed Dr. Adam. "We'll tell the police what we've found. Climb on."

Minutes later, the four-wheeler was back in the garage, and Dr. Adam was using Dora's phone to call the police. Mandy heard him telling the sergeant about the blanket and the dog food. Meanwhile, Dora lit the fire and brought out a couple of big towels so that Mandy and her dad could dry themselves off before they left.

"They're sending some men right away to do a search close to the farmhouse," Dr. Adam said when he put the phone down. "But a thorough search of the moors will have to wait until the weather lifts. Thank you, Dora," he added, taking the towel from her.

"But they *have* to do a good search!" Now that she knew Amber and Frisbee were somewhere in the area, Mandy was desperate for them to be found.

"They will the moment they're able to," her dad assured her.

"What if that moment's too late?" Mandy murmured. She took the towel Dora had brought for her and wrapped it around herself, hoping the two runaways would return to the barn for shelter.

"Come back, Amber. Please!" she whispered. "You won't get into trouble. We just want to find you!"

Five

By late that evening, the search party hadn't found any sign of Amber or Frisbee. Dora phoned Animal Ark after the police had returned to Syke Farm, drenched and shivering, saying it was too dark to keep looking. "They promised to be back with the Mooreland Rescue Team as soon as it gets light," she told Mandy. "As long as the weather doesn't get any worse."

As long as the weather doesn't get any worse! Mandy echoed silently. But what if it did? Amber and Frisbee would never survive outdoors in conditions like this. "They *must* go back to the barn tonight," she said to Dora.

"I've left a thermos of hot chocolate in case she does," said Dora, speaking quickly as if she didn't want to admit to her kindness.

Mandy could hardly sleep that night. She tossed and turned, listening to the rain pelting her window. All she could think of was the girl and the tiny puppy, alone and in danger on the bleak moor.

When gray fingers of dawn began creeping through a gap in the curtains, Mandy sprang out of bed and ran downstairs two steps at a time to phone Dora. "Are the sandwiches and hot chocolate gone?" she asked, gripping the receiver so tightly that her fingers hurt.

"No," came the curt reply.

Mandy's heart sank. "So they *have* been out on the moor all night."

"We can't be sure of that," said Dora. "They could have come back to the barn with food of their own."

"Amber dropped the puppy food," Mandy reminded her. "Frisbee must be starving by now."

"You're jumping to conclusions, Mandy. That girl's not going to let a puppy starve," said Dora. "She must have some sense in her head."

Mandy didn't agree. If Amber had any sense, she wouldn't have run off with Frisbee in the first place. She thanked Dora, hung up the phone, then flopped down in a chair and stared gloomily at the floor.

"Coming for breakfast, Mandy?" called her dad from the kitchen.

"I'm not hungry," Mandy started to answer, but she was interrupted by the phone. She grabbed it, convinced it was Dora again with good news. "Have you found them?" she asked breathlessly.

"Found who?" It was James. "Oh, you mean Amber and Frisbee? I haven't been looking for them, actually. I was calling to see if you'd heard anything yet."

When Mandy and her dad had come in last night, she'd called James to bring him up to date. Like Mandy, he'd hated the thought of the missing girl and puppy being outside all night.

"Sorry," Mandy said. "I thought you were Dora. And no, there's no good news yet." She looked out the window. It was still raining, but the sky was definitely lighter and the clouds higher. A full-scale search had to be possible this morning. But why leave it only to the professionals? The more people looking for Amber and Frisbee, the better. Mandy came to a decision. "Can you be here in fifteen minutes?"

"Sure. Why?" asked James.

"Because we're forming our own search party," Mandy replied.

"We are?" James sounded a bit surprised. "OK, I'll bring Blackie. He'll pick up their scent."

"Mmm. We'll see," muttered Mandy. If Dora's highly trained dogs hadn't been able to track Amber and Frisbee, there wasn't much hope that Blackie—the bounciest, most disobedient, but most adorable Labrador Mandy had ever known—would be any help. But he'd enjoy going out on the moor for a run. "And who knows," Mandy said to James, "Frisbee might be happy to see another dog when we find him and Amber."

"*If* we find them," said James.

"Don't be so negative," said Mandy. She put the phone down and ran upstairs to dress. Five minutes later she appeared in the kitchen.

Dr. Adam was pulling on his white coat, ready for morning clinic hours. "Going on an Arctic expedition?" he asked, surprised to see her wearing a bright red ski suit.

Mandy managed a smile. "Not unless you call the moors the Arctic." She riffled about in a heap of laundry that had just come out of the dryer and found a pair of thick thermal socks. "This is the only really bright outerwear I have. It will help us stand out on the moors if we need help. And it's definitely warm."

"Ah." Dr. Adam raised his eyebrows. "Mandy, you know the Mooreland Rescue Team will be out searching for Amber and Frisbee this morning. If they can't find them, well . . ." He stopped and shrugged. "Why am

I trying to argue with you? You'd think I'd have learned by now that it's a waste of breath trying to get you to change your mind. You're going to look for those two whatever I say, aren't you?"

Mandy nodded.

"Promise me one thing," said Dr. Adam. "That you'll be careful."

Mandy nodded again.

"And that you'll turn back if the weather gets any worse," added Dr. Emily, who was loading the dishwasher.

"Yes, yes," Mandy said impatiently. She looked out the window to see if there was any sign of James, even though she knew he'd never have gotten to Animal Ark so quickly.

"And that you'll call us if you have any trouble." Dr. Adam handed Mandy his cell phone.

"Will do," Mandy promised.

"How were you planning to get to Dora's farm?" asked Dr. Adam.

Mandy fiddled with the pair of socks in her hands. "I thought that ewe might need to have her hoof checked this morning," she said.

"Nice try, Mandy," said her mom. "Actually," Dr. Emily sounded reluctant, but she went on, "I do have to go out to see to a sick mare this morning not far from Dora's farm. I mean it, though, when I say that you're not to go too far off the beaten track. You know how dangerous it can be on the moors."

"Thanks, Mom. I promise we'll be careful." Mandy hugged Dr. Emily, who was opening a large envelope. "Are those the results of Portia's blood test?" The wording on the back flap of the envelope read *McClurg & Burrows Pathology*.

"Looks like it," said Dr. Emily. She took out the report, and she and her husband studied it in silence.

"What does it say?" Mandy asked, somehow both wanting, yet not wanting, to know the results. A diagnosis for Portia was vital, but she couldn't bear it if it turned out to be something extremely serious.

"All the tests are negative," announced Dr. Adam. "It looks like we're back to square one."

Mandy's expression fell. "But how can they all be negative when Portia's definitely sick?"

"It could be something that doesn't show up in the types of tests we ordered," explained her mom. "We're going to have to put on our thinking caps again."

Mandy bit her lip, knowing that time was running out. Her dad's words echoed in her head again: *They don't generally show signs of being sick until the illness is at a fairly advanced stage.*

Dr. Adam picked up the report and glanced through it

again. "It's probably something completely obvious that's staring us in the face."

"Then we have to stare back much harder until we see it," Mandy said with determination.

When Mandy and her mom, and James and Blackie arrived at Dora's farm forty-five minutes later, there were a number of other vehicles already parked in the yard. A blue-and-white police car stood next to two Land Rovers, one blue and the other dark green.

"Oh, good," Mandy said with relief. "The rescue team's already here." She could see them in the distance, moving in a line across the moor behind the farm. In the mist and drizzle they looked like ghosts. In happier circumstances this might have made Mandy smile. After all, it was almost Halloween. But right now, trick-or-treating was the last thing on her mind.

Watching the rescue team reminded Mandy of the time James had been lost in the Scottish Highlands. He'd fallen down a crevice on his way to get help for a stallion who was trapped at the bottom of a deep ditch. But he was quickly found thanks to a rescue dog named Moss. "It's a pity Moss is so far away. We could use a dog like that now," Mandy mused as she climbed out of the Animal Ark Land Rover.

James jumped down from the backseat with Blackie.

He looked at Mandy with a hurt expression. "I bet if Blackie was trained, he'd make an awesome search dog."

"Of course he would," Mandy agreed, although privately she thought it would take a lot of training. Blackie was adorable, but he wasn't famous for being super obedient! She gave the Labrador an affectionate pat.

Dora came out of the farmhouse then. She seemed surprised to see Mandy and her mom and James. "No news yet, I'm afraid," she told them.

"James and I have come to help," Mandy said, pulling on her gloves.

Dora looked at them doubtfully. "I don't know about that. I'm sure the team has all the manpower they need. Ten in all—two police officers and eight people from the Mooreland Search and Rescue Services."

"The more people out looking, the better," remarked James. He knelt down on one knee to tie a shoelace. Like Mandy, he was wearing hiking boots with thick rubber soles. He also had on a bulky parka that made him look twice his normal size.

"Could be," said Dora. "But you need time to catch up with them. They started out nearly an hour ago."

"We're not thinking of catching up to them," Mandy explained. "We're going to do our own search in a different area."

"One that's safe, and clearly marked," emphasized Dr. Emily.

Dora exchanged a glance with Emily Hope and shrugged. "It looks like we won't change their minds," she said. "Well, I can think of a way to help you avoid getting lost. One girl and a puppy in danger on my property is more than enough." She turned around and pointed to a crumbling stone wall snaking across the undulating moor. "See that wall?"

Mandy nodded.

"There's an old path running next to it for a couple of miles," said Dora. "The rescuers plan to get there late this afternoon. But I suppose it won't hurt if you two scout around there now."

"It looks safe enough," said James. He'd brought along a pair of binoculars and was studying the path through them.

"You'll be fine as long as you stay on the path and turn back if the weather gets worse," cautioned Dora.

Dr. Emily nodded in agreement. "It makes sense to stick to a clear path." She looked at her watch. "It's nine o'clock now. It'll take me twenty minutes to get to the Edwardses' farm and I'll be there for about half an hour. Let's meet back here at ten thirty." She was about to get into the Land Rover, but she stopped to give Mandy a hug. "You *will* be careful, won't you, honey?"

"Of course," Mandy said.

"I know I sound like a worrywart, but I can only imagine how desperate Amber's parents must be," Dr. Emily said, and sighed. "The last thing anyone needs now is for you two and Blackie to get lost as well."

"We won't," James promised.

Mandy watched her mom drive away, suddenly feeling nervous. "We'll see you in an hour and a half," she said to Dora.

"Be sure you close the gates behind you and that Blackie doesn't go near the sheep," Dora warned them.

"Don't worry about him," said James. He took a leash out of his pocket to show Dora that he could restrain Blackie if he had to.

Mandy and James set off at a fast pace for the old path, heading into an icy wind that felt as if it had come straight from the Arctic. When they came to the path Mandy crouched down and looked for footprints. But the stony ground didn't reveal any tracks.

"It looks like we'll have to rely on Blackie's nose," said James half seriously.

"I don't think that'll get us very far," Mandy remarked. "He doesn't know Amber from a bar of soap, so he's not going to get excited if he picks up her scent."

The Labrador had stopped next to a prickly clump of shrubbery several yards ahead.

"He smells something," James whispered.

Mandy had a lot of faith in dogs, but she knew Blackie well. If he'd found anything at all, it was likely to be something to eat.

James paused as Blackie pushed a branch aside to reveal an old sandwich wrapper. "False alarm." James picked the paper up and stuffed it in his pocket. "Maybe you're right, Mandy. We can't rely on Blackie completely."

A few minutes later, Blackie dove into another clump of bushes. He let out a sharp bark of triumph, and Mandy's heart lurched. Had he found some trace of Amber and Frisbee?

The two friends sprinted down the path and had almost reached Blackie when a small brown creature shot out in front of them and darted away.

Mandy stopped running. "Another false alarm!" she said gloomily.

The terrified rabbit bounded across the moor with Blackie in hot pursuit.

"Blackie!" yelled James, chasing after him.

The rabbit scurried down a hole, and James managed to reach Blackie before he started trying to dig it out. "That's enough!" he scolded. "We're looking for a girl and a puppy. Not bunnies." He tugged the leash but the Labrador stayed put. "Sometimes," James said, feeling in his pocket, "you're more stubborn than a mule." He took out a dog biscuit and used it to lure Blackie back to the path. "Now, can we please concentrate on finding Amber and Frisbee?"

They continued along the path, checking behind the wall every now and then to see if Amber was huddled behind it.

"Amber!" Mandy called out several times. "It's OK! You're not in trouble! Your mom and dad only want to know that you're safe!" But her cries were met with silence.

"She *has* to be out here somewhere," said James, scanning the hills with his binoculars.

On the horizon, big black clouds were building up once more, and the steady drizzle that had been falling for the past hour was getting heavier. Mandy could just make out the other search party high on the moor across the valley. If she hadn't known what the distant gray shapes were, she'd have mistaken them for rocks or shrubs.

"There's nothing here!" Mandy sighed. "Not even a candy wrapper." It seemed as if Amber and Frisbee had vanished into thin air, leaving only a blanket and a half-eaten packet of puppy food. She looked at her watch. It was nearly ten o'clock! "We'll have to start back," she told James reluctantly.

"OK." He was studying the moor one last time through his binoculars. "Let's hope the others have better luck." He whistled to Blackie, who was sniffing at another hole, probably in the hope of scaring out another rabbit. "Come on, boy. We're going home."

Blackie ignored him.

"Blackie!" repeated James.

At that moment, Mandy glimpsed a second rabbit crouched next to a bush not far from the Labrador. *Please don't move*, she willed the little animal. Another chase across the moor would delay them even more. But the creature's flight reflex kicked in, and it darted off like a little brown missile.

Blackie charged across the moor behind it, his ears flapping in the wind and his tail stretched out.

"Blackie!" shouted James, racing after him.

The rabbit ran up a short hill and vanished down a hole near the top. But Blackie thundered right past. Either he hadn't seen the hole or he was on the trail of something else.

"Now what?" James puffed, running faster. Ahead of him, Blackie paused to sniff the ground before disappearing down the other side of the slope.

Mandy caught up with James just as he reached the top of the hill. They stopped to catch their breath and watched Blackie running at full speed across the moor.

He was heading in a straight line toward a tumbledown stone shed half hidden by a grove of trees.

"Maybe they're . . ." Mandy started to say, just as James said, "You don't think . . ."

Understanding each other perfectly, the two friends raced down the hill.

"It's probably just another rabbit," Mandy said, panting.

Running too fast to speak, James nodded.

Blackie stopped near the building then, and started to sniff around the walls. Seen close up, the building was even more run-down than Mandy had first thought. The walls were crumbling, and most of the slate roof had fallen in. A wooden door hung on one hinge and swung back and forth in the wind.

"It must be about as sheltered in there as it is outside," Mandy remarked, raising her voice above the howling wind.

"Let's look inside anyway," suggested James.

"OK. But hold on to Blackie in case he was after another rabbit," Mandy warned. She heaved the door open and slipped inside. She paused, waiting for her eyes to adjust to the darkness. There was a smell of damp earth and mold, and the stone floor was scattered with old straw.

James and Blackie squeezed in behind her. "It's not

exactly the most welcoming sort of place," remarked James.

An icy draft whistled around Mandy as she took a few steps forward. She could just make out a pile of old hay bales heaped in a corner. But that wasn't all. "What's that?" she whispered.

At the bottom of the stack was a long, low lump, just about the size and shape of a sleeping person. Mandy caught her breath. It *was* a person! There was a girl curled up, fast asleep on the hay-strewn floor. She was wearing a blue jacket and clutching a large backpack in her arms. Her long dark hair fell over her cheek, and her fingers looked very white against the navy blue fabric of the rucksack.

Mandy knelt down to get a closer look and saw that the flap of the backpack was twitching. Carefully, she lifted it up. "Oh!" she whispered when a little face popped out—a sweet, brown-and-white face framed by soft, drooping brown ears. The face of a beagle puppy.

"It's Amber and Frisbee!" Mandy said softly.

Six

The puppy stretched his neck and licked Mandy's hand. His tiny pink tongue felt warm and velvety. Then he wriggled out of the backpack and into Mandy's out-stretched arms.

"You're absolutely gorgeous!" she said, cuddling him. She spoke quietly, not wanting to wake Amber. "Can you believe it?" she whispered to James, who was smiling from ear to ear.

"I knew Blackie would find them!" he murmured proudly, patting his dog. Mandy had her arms wrapped around the puppy so that he was hidden from Blackie's

view, but the Labrador's sharp nose had picked up
Frisbee's scent and he was sniffing the air curiously.

Mandy held the beagle up in front of her to get a good
look at him.

"He looks like he's in good shape," James observed.
"Amber's obviously been taking good care of him."

Mandy hardly heard him. She was staring in horror at
the beagle. "But look at his eye, James!" she gasped.

An ugly pink lump about the size of a marble filled the
inside corner of the puppy's right eye. It looked both
painful and awkward. Mandy couldn't remember seeing
anything like it before.

Mandy's shocked outburst woke Amber up. "What do
you want?" she cried, sitting up. She saw Frisbee in
Mandy's arms. "Give him to me! He's mine!" she shouted,
and before Mandy knew it, Amber had grabbed the
puppy and was scrambling to her feet.

"It's OK," Mandy said, standing up, too. "We want to
help you." She glanced at the puppy's painful-looking
eye and added, "And Frisbee."

"We don't need any help!" Amber insisted, and she
covered the puppy's face with one hand. "Just leave
us alone!" She looked very pale, and Mandy saw that
her fingers were shaking. Her hair was lank and dirty,
and there was a grubby mark on her cheek from where
she'd been lying on the rotten straw. She'd obviously

watched over Frisbee, but she hadn't taken care of herself at all.

Blackie jumped up at Frisbee, wagging his tail.

"Whoa, boy!" James said, gripping Blackie's collar with both hands.

Amber backed up against the hay and clutched the beagle closer. "Keep that dog away! I don't want him to hurt Frisbee."

"Don't worry. Blackie would never hurt a puppy," James assured her. "He only wants to say hello," he added.

"Well, he can't," said Amber, edging farther away. "He might . . ."

"Hurt Frisbee's eye?" Mandy quietly ended the sentence for her.

Amber said nothing. She half turned, as if shielding Frisbee. "Just leave us alone," she murmured. "Please!" Frisbee wriggled in her arms. She petted him and whispered something in his velvety floppy ear. Then she lifted the flap of the backpack and gently put Frisbee inside so that only his head was visible.

Seeing him peeping out in that way reminded Mandy of something she'd once read about beagles—that hunters in the eighteenth century used to work with tiny beagles who could fit inside their hunting coat pockets. "He's a pocket beagle," Mandy said with a smile.

"What do you mean?" Amber demanded, shooting Mandy a worried look.

"It's a name given to very small beagles," Mandy explained.

"But Frisbee's not small for his age!" Amber blurted out. "His brothers and sisters were exactly the same size. There's nothing wrong with him."

"I think there is," James replied. "But it's not his size. It's his eye."

His bluntness made Amber even more defensive. "He's fine," she protested, but Mandy could tell by the catch in her voice that Amber didn't really believe this.

"Look, Amber," Mandy said. "Everyone's very worried about you. Your mom's been on TV begging you to come home."

Amber looked amazed. "Really?"

"She just wants to know you're safe," added James.

"Well, I am," said Amber.

"No one knows that yet, except for us. And you must realize that Frisbee needs to get to a vet soon," Mandy pointed out.

The puppy blinked at Mandy as if he was agreeing with her.

"There's a Mooreland Search and Rescue Team close by, with the police," said James. "They'll be able to take you home right away."

"The police!" Amber tightened her grip on the backpack. Frisbee shook his ears with a flap, as if he didn't want to be squashed. "Am I in trouble?" Amber whispered.

"No, they're just out looking for you," James told her. "I can run and tell them we've found you while you go to the farmhouse with Mandy to wait for her mom. Dr. Emily's a vet."

The mention of a vet seemed to upset Amber even more than news of the police looking for her. "We can't go to a vet," she sobbed, tears welling up in her eyes. "I won't let anyone put Frisbee to sleep," and without another word, she raced over to the door and slipped outside.

"Wait!" Mandy cried. She started to run after her just as Blackie yanked himself free from James, who toppled over on the slippery straw. The leash slipped out of James's hands and Blackie bounded forward, straight into Mandy's legs. "Oof!" she gasped, losing her balance and crashing onto the stack of bales.

Luckily, James's years of practice catching Blackie had prepared him. Though he was sprawled out on his stomach, he managed to grab the end of the leash before Blackie could charge away. "Got you!" he said, springing to his feet.

Mandy was up in a flash, too. "We have to stop Amber!"

she shouted, and ran outside to find that the big black clouds had finally burst. Raindrops streamed from the sky like a thick gray curtain.

"Come on, James!" Mandy urged, shielding her eyes against the rain to gaze across the field behind the shed. Amber was a surprisingly fast runner, and she was already clambering over a wall far ahead. With Blackie racing at the end of his leash, they rushed after her.

"Stop!" Mandy yelled. "We only want to help you." But either her voice was swallowed up by the rain and wind or Amber was deliberately ignoring her, because the girl ahead of them started running again after she cleared the wall.

"We'll never catch her." Mandy puffed. She lengthened her stride as Amber scrambled over another wall and began to race up the rocky land of the open moor.

Then Mandy blinked.

Amber had vanished! It was as if she'd been plucked off the moor and spirited away.

"Where did she go?" James yelled above the wind. He held up his free hand to push the wet hair out of his eyes, but his glasses were so wet with raindrops that Mandy doubted he could see any better.

They reached the wall at the edge of the field and hoisted themselves over; Blackie cleared it with an enormous leap that almost wrenched James's arm out of its socket. They ran on up the hill until they came to the point where Amber and Frisbee had disappeared. Mandy looked around. Amber couldn't have dived behind a rock or clump of bushes. Apart from a few flat boulders, the bleak, soggy landscape was empty.

"How can someone just evaporate?" said James. He took off his glasses and wiped them on the hem of his jacket. Clean glasses or not, there was still no sign of Amber when he put them on again.

Blackie was just as confused. He turned around and around, his broad black face creased in a frown. Mandy was about to suggest that James let him go. He'd led them to the runaways once before; he could probably do it again.

And then, above the wind, came a faint cry. "Help!"

It was Amber! It sounded like she was a long way away.

The chase across the moor had left Mandy feeling hot inside her ski suit, but a cold shiver ran through her as Amber cried out again. "Help me! Please!"

"This is really weird," whispered James, staring around them at the empty moor. Mandy guessed he was thinking about Halloween and unexplained supernatural phenomena.

"Help, someone! Help!" The desperate plea seemed to swim up from the ground, muffled yet echoing, like someone calling from under the sea.

"Where are you?" Mandy yelled as loud as she could.

"Over here!" came the distant reply.

James scratched his head. "It's crazy. She sounds near *and* far away."

It was like a riddle. But one that Mandy knew had to be solved fast. "Where's 'here'?" Mandy shouted again, then listened hard for the reply.

"Down here!"

That meant Amber was either at the bottom of a hill—but Mandy could see for miles around, and there was no sign of a girl or a puppy in a backpack—or she was *underground*.

James slowly walked on again, with Blackie leaping and squirming at the end of the leash like a fish on a line. Suddenly, he stopped. "Look!" he said, pointing to a rock in front of him.

Mandy ran over. Almost hidden by the rock was a jagged black hole about the size of a foxhole. Her hands flew up to her mouth. Amber *was* underground.

Mandy hadn't seen many potholes before but she knew that these entrances to underground caves were dotted all over the moor. They were often fenced off by farmers who were worried about losing sheep. If Amber had really fallen into one, she could be in big, big trouble.

"I hope it's not too deep," said James, echoing Mandy's

thoughts. He knelt down and peered into the darkness. "Amber? Are you OK?"

"I th-th-think so," came Amber's muted voice.

"And Frisbee?" Mandy braced herself for the reply.

There was another pause. Mandy bit her lip. She imagined the worst—like Amber landing on top of Frisbee in his backpack, crushing him beneath her. Or Frisbee being flung out and crashing into the rocks. At best, he'd be cut and bruised and very frightened. She exchanged a worried glance with James.

"He's fine."

Mandy almost fell over with relief.

"The backpack must have protected him," Amber continued.

Mandy remembered that the pack was thickly padded. It probably also contained a few items of clothing that would have added to the padding. "Can you climb out?" she called to Amber. She looked down, hoping to see her. But all she could see was a narrow tunnel sloping down at an angle and surrounded by steep, rocky walls.

"I'll try." There was another pause, then Amber said, "Ah! My ankle hurts! I think it's sprained."

This was all they needed! Mandy thought fast. "Dad's phone!" she remembered, and reached into her pocket.

It wasn't there! She struck her forehead with her

hand. "I can't believe it!" she told James. "I left it at home!" There was only one other option. "You've got to go for help, James. I'm going down to see if I can help Amber."

"You can't do that!" James protested, his face white under his dripping hair. "It's too dangerous!"

Mandy looked back at him. "Imagine how Amber must be feeling," she said quietly so that Amber wouldn't hear her. "She needs company more than anything else. And don't forget Frisbee. He must be scared, and his eye must be hurting, too. I could help by keeping him calm." She pushed James's arm. "Go on, run!"

Before James could say anything else, Mandy wriggled into the hole and clung to the edge while her feet searched for a foothold on the walls. "I'm coming down, Amber," she called.

"Be careful, Mandy," James said while Blackie whined softly and nuzzled Mandy's head.

"I'll be fine," Mandy promised, hoping she sounded more confident than she felt. "Now go."

"OK," said James. "I'll be as quick as I can."

Mandy listened to the soft thudding of his feet and felt the vibrations on the ground as he ran away. Then she braced her feet against the slippery sides of the tunnel and started to inch her way down. Her nails scraped against the rocky wall, and she could feel moss and dirt collecting beneath them. The tunnel curved around before plunging straight down, getting narrower all the time. Mandy's heart thudded uncomfortably. It was like going down a funnel. She looked up and saw the tiniest slit of gray sky above her. She was probably only about a yard or so below the surface, but already it felt like she was deep underground. "Are you still OK, Amber?" she called.

"Uh-huh." Amber sounded very close now. "But watch out. There's a big rock jutting out just behind you."

"Thanks," Mandy said, and she felt the rock scrape her back as she lowered herself past it. Her feet touched a hard, flat surface. She'd reached the bottom. "Phew!" she said.

Amber was sitting on the floor of a small cave with one leg — probably the injured one — stretched out, and the other tucked underneath her. She hugged the backpack to her, protecting the precious contents.

There was just enough light filtering down the tunnel for Mandy to see around the cave. When she looked back up at the way she'd come, she realized with a gulp that it was completely sheer and would be hard enough to climb up without an injured ankle. There was no way out now, not until the rescue team arrived. Fighting back the urge to panic, she crouched down next to Amber.

"I guess I should introduce myself," said Mandy, trying to make out the expression on Amber's face. "I'm Mandy Hope."

"Hi, again," the scared-looking girl replied. "I'm Amber—"

"I know," said Mandy. "Actually, the whole county knows." She could see now that Amber smiled at her joke, and looked a little less intimidated.

"At least you're both more or less all right," Mandy said.

Amber edged to one side of the cave to give Mandy a little more space. There was just enough room for the two of them. There was a small hole in the opposite wall, and when Mandy peered through it she saw that it was another narrow tunnel. "Not much good going in there. It's even more cramped," she murmured, already feeling claustrophobic. "James will be back with help soon," she told Amber.

Frisbee must have recognized her voice because he peeped out of the backpack. He squirmed with delight when he saw Mandy and worked his way out onto her lap. Amber didn't seem to mind him being friendly to someone else.

"Hi, again," Mandy smiled, hugging him. "It's good to see you. She tried to sound cheerful, but even to her own ears her voice seemed strained. The hideous lump in Frisbee's eye made the fall into the pothole seem minor.

Amber must have noticed the tension in Mandy's voice. She reached over and petted Frisbee, who had curled up in Mandy's arms. "He's just the best, you know?"

Mandy nodded but said nothing. She had a feeling Amber was about to tell her a lot more. She had climbed down the pothole to help, and if listening was the best way to do that, then she was all ears.

"I adored him the moment I saw him," Amber went on, not taking her eyes off Frisbee's floppy ears. "He was always the first to run to me when I arrived."

The puppy rolled over and lay on his back in Mandy's arms. Mandy ran her fingers up and down his little round belly, and Frisbee grunted with pleasure.

"He loves that," said Amber. "And chasing balls, and digging holes . . ." She gulped, and Mandy realized she was fighting back tears.

"I just can't let him be put to sleep," Amber said in a rush before she finally broke down. "It would be like putting down my best friend," she sobbed.

Mandy didn't know what to say. Frisbee appeared to be the picture of health—until you saw his eye. She had to admit that the pink tumor looked very serious, serious enough to be inoperable. For once, she couldn't offer any comforting words about the great things her parents could do to help sick animals.

Amber put her hands over her face. "We can't let him die."

Hot tears burned Mandy's cheeks, too. She shifted Frisbee into the crook of one arm and put the other around Amber's shoulders. "I know how you feel," she murmured. "I've loved so many gorgeous animals that my mom and dad couldn't help. It's really tough, but I've had to learn that sometimes the best thing we can do for an animal who's seriously ill is . . ." She trailed off.

Amber was silent, waiting for Mandy to finish.

"Is to release them from their misery." Mandy's whispered words bounced around the walls of the cave like a clock striking the hour. With a painful lump in her throat, she kissed the top of Frisbee's head, wondering just how much time he had left.

Frisbee stretched luxuriously, then rolled over and scrambled onto Mandy's lap. She wriggled her finger in front of him, and he dabbed at it with a front paw before he jumped down and started pulling at Amber's shoelaces with his teeth.

"See what I mean? He's got so much energy," said Amber, looking at Mandy again. "It's not like he's in any pain. And that's why I had to take him away."

Mandy wasn't sure she followed Amber's drift. "What do you mean?"

"The sanctuary was really busy, and when Frisbee and his brothers and sisters were brought in, Linda Davis—the woman who runs the kennels—asked me to be in charge of them. So no one else really got to see them right away," explained Amber. "Which was good."

Mandy was still perplexed. It must have shown on her face because Amber continued. "If other people had seen Frisbee's eye, they'd have called in a vet. And then he'd have been put to sleep by now." She winced as Frisbee attacked the shoe on her injured foot. But she didn't stop him from playing. It seemed she was prepared to suffer anything for him.

"You can't be sure of that," Mandy argued, wishing she hadn't said anything about animals being put out of their misery. "Didn't you think there might be a chance a vet could help Frisbee recover?"

"I couldn't take the chance," said Amber. "One of my friends had a puppy with eye cancer. As soon as the vet knew what the problem was, he put the puppy down. I wanted Frisbee to have a chance at life."

Mandy finally understood why Amber had run away. Who wouldn't want such a lively, adorable puppy to live? "You're right," she said, wrenching the words out from somewhere deep inside. "Frisbee deserves to have a great life. But he also deserves to have whatever veterinary treatment he needs." With a jolt, she thought about Portia and her dad saying that birds pretended they weren't sick even when they really were. What if Frisbee's eyes were hurting, but being a puppy who loved to play, he didn't give in to the pain? She kept quiet, guessing that wasn't something Amber would want to hear. It was better that she thought her beloved pup was genuinely happy in spite of the growth in his eye.

For a while, neither of them spoke. Frisbee gave up wrestling with their shoelaces and climbed onto Amber's lap where he started to bite at the zipper of her jacket. Amber tickled his chest. "You don't think . . ." she trailed off, not looking at Mandy.

"Think what?"

"That I'm being cruel, keeping him away from a vet?"

"Not deliberately cruel," Mandy said. She didn't want to heap any blame on Amber. "You did what you thought was right for him."

"Mmm, but maybe I should—" Amber broke off sharply. "Listen! Can you hear that?"

"What?" Mandy strained her ears, and heard a faint rushing noise. It sounded like wind, and it was coming from the little tunnel on the far side of the cave. "I'll go check it out," she volunteered. "It could be another opening outside." She squeezed through the hole in the rock and, feeling her way with difficulty, crawled along the dark tunnel as fast as she could.

The stone floor was cold and damp so that her hands, even inside her gloves, were soon burning. So were her knees. Once, she bumped her head hard on the low roof and when she rubbed it, she felt the sticky dampness of blood. She reminded herself that cut scalps always bled more than anywhere else and forced herself to keep going.

All the while, the rushing sound grew louder.

After several yards the tunnel divided in two, but Mandy pushed on, following the direction the noise was coming from. Eventually, after crawling for what seemed like miles, but was probably only about fifty feet, she came across something that made her turn ice-cold.

It wasn't wind they'd heard, but water.

The tunnel opened out halfway up one side of a shallow cave that stretched on either side as far as Mandy could see in the dim light. And rushing across the floor of the cave, swirling and glinting and swelling farther up the wall to their level in the tunnel, was a fast-moving underground river.

Seven

"We've got to get out of here!" Mandy gasped. She'd crawled back along the tunnel as fast as she could, this time hitting her forehead on a protruding rock. Her skin stung but there was no time to stop. The river was rising fast, fed by the torrential rain from above.

"The river's flooding. We have to get out!" Mandy said urgently.

Amber stared at her in alarm. "How?" She glanced at her ankle. "I've already tried once."

"We'll have to climb out," said Mandy. "I'll help you. And I'll carry Frisbee in the backpack."

She took the bag from Amber, gently put Frisbee

inside, then eased it over her shoulders. The puppy
didn't protest. Having traveled inside the backpack for
a few days, he must have felt quite at home in there.

A born pocket beagle, Mandy thought. She held out
her hand and helped Amber up. As soon as Amber was
on her feet, she sucked in her breath and stumbled
against the rocky wall, taking the weight off her injured
ankle.

Mandy stared at the vertical rock face above them.
Could they really climb out? Amber's ankle was obviously really sore. But they had no choice. The sound of
rushing water was getting louder. Soon it would start
seeping into the cave.

"You go first," Mandy said. "You can use me as a foothold."

Standing on her good leg, Amber reached up and
gripped a small ledge that jutted out from the slippery
rock face. She tried to pull herself up with her arms, but
couldn't. She put her injured foot on a bulging rock and
bravely tried to haul herself up, but the moment she put
weight on her injured ankle, she cried out in pain and
fell to the floor. "I can't do it!"

Mandy's heart sank. She looked up again, desperately
hoping to see the faces of the rescue party, but all she
saw against the slit of gray sky was the rain streaming
down through the opening.

Amber huddled up against the side of the cave. "This is all my fault," she said, sobbing.

Mandy said nothing. She was busy trying to come up with another plan.

"You climb out, Mandy. You and Frisbee," continued Amber.

Her words shattered Mandy's concentration. "And leave you here?" she exclaimed. "I'd never do that."

"It's your only chance," insisted Amber. "Frisbee's, too."

Above the sound of the rising river came a new noise, like a tap being turned on and left to run. It could mean only one thing: Water had started to flow along the tunnel toward them. But it was only when Mandy saw a narrow stream trickling through the entrance to the tunnel that she realized just how close it was. "It's coming in here already!" she said, trying not to panic.

Suddenly, she remembered the fork in the tunnel. Perhaps it would lead them away from the water. Wherever it went, it was their only hope. "Do you think you can crawl, Amber?"

"I'm sure I can."

"Good. Follow me." Mandy dropped onto her hands and knees and heaved the backpack around so that it hung underneath her, like a kangaroo's pouch. "Just hang in there, little one," she murmured to Frisbee.

Then she started up the tunnel once more. She tried to stay calm but her nerves were fried. They could be heading into even more serious trouble with every move.

The water coursing along the tunnel floor soon became a shallow stream, covering Mandy's hands and knees. It was ice-cold, but she was less worried about the temperature than about the depth. It wouldn't be long before the water came up to the backpack and started to cover Frisbee.

"Are you all right?" she shouted to Amber.

"Yes."

"Can you go faster?"

"Maybe."

Mandy dug deep and found a reserve of speed and strength she didn't know she had. Her legs and arms swished through the water so that she was half swimming down the tunnel. She could hear Amber splashing through the rising stream just inches behind.

By the time Mandy reached the fork, the water was halfway up her thighs and arms, washing against the backpack and dragging at the sodden fabric. "Head left here," she shouted to Amber.

The second tunnel was as narrow as the first and seemed to be equally level, so for a while they were still crawling along in rapidly rising water. It was pitch-dark in this tunnel, whereas there had at least been a glimmer of daylight seeping into the first. She tried not to think about what would happen if this tunnel led nowhere— or worse, took them deeper underground, nearer the level of the river.

After a few minutes, Mandy's arms and legs seemed to be moving more freely, as though the water had gotten shallower. Was it just wishful thinking? She patted the bottom of the backpack. It was wet, but it was definitely above the waterline. "The water's dropping!" she cried triumphantly.

"It's not," said Amber. "We're going uphill. The water hasn't reached this high yet."

Amber was right. Mandy could feel the ground getting steeper. Was this good news? What if the tunnel ended in another sheer rock wall?

Frisbee was growing restless. Mandy could feel him squirming inside the backpack, but there was nothing she could do to help.

Just when Mandy thought she couldn't crawl another inch, she saw something that gave her courage. The darkness in the tunnel ahead was sort of hazy, as if it had been pierced by a glimmer of light. Mandy blinked, and when the faint light remained, she felt a shiver of excitement. "There's a light at the end of the tunnel!" she called, and despite the danger they'd been in—or perhaps because of it—she burst out laughing and repeated the well-worn phrase.

After another hundred feet of uncomfortable crawling, they found themselves in another cave, bigger than the first but with the same sheer, slippery walls. Mandy stood up. It felt so good to be back on her feet. "We made it!" she shouted at the top of her voice. She took off the backpack and put it on the ground, then lifted Frisbee out and hugged him tightly. What a brave puppy!

Amber sat on the floor and leaned against the rocky wall. She smiled up at Mandy. "See what I mean? He's amazing."

"He is," Mandy agreed. It was too early to celebrate, though. They were out of immediate danger, but they were, in a sense, back to square one. Amber was stuck underground with a badly injured ankle, and not far below was an underground river in flood.

Mandy looked up at the pothole in the far corner of the cave ceiling. It looked bigger than the first hole, but it was also a lot higher. Mandy shielded her eyes from the sky, which, after the darkness in the narrow tunnel, seemed very bright. Suddenly, she realized that it had stopped raining—there were no drops falling down from the hole. Still, there was no time to waste. "Wait here," she said to Amber.

"I wasn't planning on going anywhere," Amber said wryly.

Mandy grinned. "I'm going to see if there's any sign of James yet. He must have reached the rescue team by now." She put Frisbee in Amber's lap then inspected the rocky sides of the pothole, looking for the best way out. But the walls were as smooth as glass, even more difficult to climb than the walls of the first cave. There wasn't a single foothold.

Mandy slumped down next to Amber. "It looks like I'm going nowhere, too." Panic started to rise in her again. "We've got to hope that James and the others look for more potholes when they find we're not in the first one."

"They will," said Amber. But her worried expression and the fear in her voice gave away her real feelings.

Frisbee was sniffing around the backpack, trying to lift the flap with his little black nose.

"He's hungry," said Amber. She reached into the bag and took out a packet of dog food—the same brand that Mandy had found on Dora's farm. Amber poured some of it into her hand. "This is the last bag of food. But don't worry, Frisbee," she added. "They'll come and get us soon. You won't go hungry." She glanced up at Mandy, her eyes troubled. "Linda's going to be so angry with me. She owns the rescue center. I mean, I stole Frisbee, didn't I? Do you think I'll be arrested?"

Mandy shook her head. "I don't think so," she said, hoping she was right. "Linda will understand that you were only trying to help Frisbee." Amber looked so worried that Mandy felt a pang of sympathy for her. Mandy realized that she had found a soul mate! Despite everything she'd been through and the danger they were still in, Amber's chief concern was for the puppy, not for herself.

Mandy couldn't think of anything more comforting to say so she scooped out some biscuits from the packet of dog food and held her cupped hand next to Amber's. Frisbee polished them off in a flash.

"He's got a good appetite," Mandy said. She offered him another handful, and he was halfway through it when he suddenly stopped eating.

"Full already?" Mandy teased.

Frisbee ignored her. He was staring ahead, his forehead creased in a frown.

"He's listening to something," whispered Amber.

Mandy was impressed. Amber certainly knew the puppy well. Frisbee lifted his nose and looked up. Mandy followed his gaze and saw a dark shape appear over the hole. It was the shape of a head. A dog's head!

"Blackie!" Mandy cried. "You've found us, you smart boy!"

Blackie looked over his shoulder and barked until a second face appeared. James!

"There you are!" he cried. "We thought something terrible had happened. The other hole's full of water."

"Something terrible nearly did happen!" Mandy told him. She tried not to picture the flooded pothole.

"How did you get here?" asked James.

"It's a long story. I'll tell you later," Mandy called up to him. She was suddenly aware of how cold and wet she was, and when she glanced at Amber, she noticed that her face was deathly pale. Even Frisbee was shivering. Mandy picked him up and cuddled him closely.

"Hang on. The search team's coming over right now with ropes and things," said James, and he looked away to signal to someone aboveground.

The rescue that followed was like something Mandy had seen on TV but never dreamed could happen to her. A rope was lowered into the pothole, and a member of the Mooreland Rescue Team rappelled swiftly down. With his bright orange overalls and yellow helmet, it was only when he was standing right in front of her that Mandy recognized who it was. "Mr. Hardy!" she exclaimed. "What are you doing here?"

"What do you think I'm doing here?" said a smiling Julian Hardy, slipping off his backpack. "Bringing you some refreshments from the Fox and Goose?" Instead of a lemonade and some pretzels, he was carrying a first-aid kit and a harness. "I joined the Mooreland Rescue Team at the end of the summer. This is my first rescue," he explained as he opened the kit and checked Amber's ankle before seeing if she had any other injuries. When he was satisfied that she could be moved, he said, "I think we can hoist you up now," and he strapped her into the harness. Supporting her so that she didn't have to put any weight on her bad ankle, Mr. Hardy tugged on the rope and called to someone aboveground. "You can lift her out now!"

Slowly, Amber was hauled to the surface where someone helped her away from the pothole. Moments later, the harness was lowered into the hole again.

"Your turn now," said Julian to Mandy. He noticed the gash above her eye. "That doesn't look too good."

"It's nothing," Mandy insisted. "I'll be fine." She petted Frisbee, who was looking up at her, the pink tumor half filling his eye. A big lump formed in her throat. If only she could be sure that he was going to be fine, too.

She put Frisbee into the backpack again, then clutched it firmly while Julian strapped her into the harness. He made sure it was properly fastened before tugging on the rope. "She's ready," he called to his help aboveground.

"Going up," Mandy said to Frisbee as the harness pulled tight around her and her feet lifted off the ground.

Below her, Julian Hardy stood with his hands on his hips while he watched her being pulled to safety.

"Careful!" she heard someone say as her head bumped against the rim of the hole. Strong hands reached in and grasped her elbows, then eased her out of the hole and onto firm ground. Mandy stood blinking for a moment, dazzled by the sudden daylight.

She was aware of someone unclipping the rope from the harness and draping a thick blanket over her shoulders. Suddenly, a familiar figure rushed up and flung his arms around her.

"You're safe!" James exclaimed. And then, as if he was embarrassed, he turned away to look at the rescue van as if it were the most interesting thing he'd ever seen. Amber was sitting in the back, having her ankle wrapped by a member of the rescue team. There was a blanket over her shoulders, and Mandy noticed that her jacket and jeans were muddy and torn. She glanced down at her ski suit; it was just as filthy and both knees were ripped open.

A policeman handed Amber a cell phone and quietly said something to her. She nodded, then hesitated a moment before punching in some numbers and putting the phone to her ear.

James took off his glasses and studied them closely before rubbing off a very stubborn but invisible smudge.

"So you're all OK?" he said at last, putting his glasses back on. "Frisbee, too?"

"I think so," Mandy said, feeling a little dazed. She could feel Frisbee moving around inside the backpack.

She looked at Amber again and saw the girl bite her lip before saying, "Hello, Mom?" Tears started to pour down her cheeks. "I'm fine," she whispered into the phone. "I'm really sorry. Please tell Linda Davis that I never meant to hurt Frisbee. I only took him because I wanted to have a chance to take care of him." She started to cry so hard that the police officer took the phone from her.

"Just a badly sprained ankle from the look of it, Mrs. Hutton," Mandy heard him say. "We'll take her to Walton Hospital and meet you there."

Amber stared at him through her tears and shook her head violently.

Mandy wondered what Amber meant. Then her attention was drawn away as one of the rescuers came over to help her out of the harness so that it could be lowered to Julian in the pothole.

Frisbee was struggling so much that the flap of the backpack opened. He peered out and spotted Blackie, who was sitting beside James. The little puppy barked, and Mandy felt his tiny tail thudding against the inside of the bag. It wasn't the normal bark of a dog but a

baying sound that immediately identified him as a
hound. He wriggled until Mandy lifted him out and put
him on the ground.

Blackie dropped to his belly. With surprising gentle-
ness, he nudged the little beagle with his nose. Then he
flopped over to his side and lay still while the puppy
crawled all over him.

"He seems fine," said James, sounding very relieved.
He felt around in his pocket. "But I bet he's hungry."

Mandy didn't have the heart to tell him that Frisbee
had had a big meal in the cave. But Frisbee scarfed
down the treat as if it were the first thing he'd eaten
in days.

"Typical beagle!" she called from her seat in the back
of the rescue van. "They're real gluttons."

"Just like Labradors," volunteered James, handing a
treat to Blackie so that he wouldn't feel left out.

Mandy was about to say something about not letting
Frisbee get too fat but the sight of the tumor in his eye
stopped her. What did it matter if he ate too much? *We
should let him enjoy life while he has the chance*, she
thought.

Mandy sat in silence on the drive back to Dora's farmhouse. Even the throbbing cut on her forehead couldn't
stop her from worrying about what was going to happen to the puppy. It looked as if Amber was having

similar thoughts as she cuddled Frisbee on her lap. Mandy reached out and squeezed her arm, wanting her to know that she hated the uncertainty about the puppy's future as much as Amber did.

Dr. Emily was waiting anxiously for them in the farmyard. She ran over to meet the van, flung open Mandy's door, and hugged her so tightly she could hardly breathe. "Thank goodness, you're all safe!"

She stepped back to let Mandy climb out and noticed the cut on her forehead. She brushed away Mandy's bangs for a closer look and said with a frown, "That's probably going to need a stitch or two. We'll have to get you to the hospital." Then, seeing Julian Hardy lift Amber out on the other side, she added, "You, too, Amber."

Amber shook her head. "I'm not going near a hospital. Not until . . ." She swallowed hard and looked down at the sleeping puppy in her arms.

"Until what?" prompted Dr. Emily.

"Until you've taken care of Frisbee," Mandy said quietly.

Eight

Mugs of steaming hot chocolate helped to warm them all up. Dora had run inside to prepare it as soon as she saw the van coming down from the moor. Everyone crowded into the living room and drank the cocoa in front of the blazing fire.

Mandy solved the problem of Amber's refusal to go to the hospital by suggesting that she go back to Animal Ark with her and her mom and James. "Mr. and Mrs. Hutton can meet her there, then take her to hospital," she said.

The police sergeant called Amber's parents. They agreed to the plan when he assured them she didn't seem to be hurt apart from her ankle. Satisfied that Amber was in good hands, the rescue team and police officers started to leave. Just as Julian was about to close the door, Amber called out to him. "Thank you, Mr. Hardy!" she said. "Thank you for everything."

Julian smiled at her. "I think James deserves the thanks. He's the one who found you."

"Me?" James shook his head. He pointed at Blackie, who was lying in front of the fire. "He's the real hero."

Once the rescue team had left, Mandy's mom picked up Frisbee to have a look at him. "Let's see what the problem is," she said, sitting on a chair with the puppy in her lap.

Mandy and Amber sat side by side on the sofa, watching. Frisbee wriggled and wagged his tail as if he thought this was a game.

"You're not helping me, little fella," Dr. Emily said, smiling. "You've got to sit still."

"I'll hold him for you," Mandy offered.

"It's all right," said her mom. "I can't do a thorough examination without the right instruments. I'll wait until we get back to the clinic."

Amber was sitting on the edge of the sofa chewing her nails. "Do you have any idea what's wrong with him?"

"Possibly. But I don't want to say anything until I know for certain," replied Dr. Emily.

Mandy bit her lip. Was this because her mom didn't want to get their hopes up — or because the truth would be too upsetting for them to deal with?

It was nearly time for afternoon clinic hours when they returned to Animal Ark. Dr. Adam hurried out when he heard the Land Rover coming up the driveway.

"You're very lucky," he said when Mandy climbed out of the vehicle. His voice was muffled against her hair as he hugged her. Dr. Emily had called him from the farmhouse when she knew that Mandy and Amber were safe, so he'd heard all about their narrow escape. "You could have drowned."

"I guess so," Mandy said, not wanting to think about the way things could have turned out.

Dr. Adam helped Amber out of the Land Rover and carried her up the steps into the waiting room. Mandy had a patient to carry in, too — Frisbee — while James tied Blackie to the porch and gave him a handful of treats to keep him happy.

"I'll call your parents to say you're here," Dr. Adam told Amber, settling her in a chair. "They'll want to take you right to Walton Hospital to have that ankle treated."

Amber shook her head. "I'm not going anywhere. I'm staying with Frisbee until" — she stopped and swallowed hard, then looked at the puppy in Mandy's arms—"at least until I know what's wrong with him. Then I need to call Linda and tell her everything."

"I guess you're not going anywhere, either, Mandy," said her dad, frowning at the cut on her forehead.

"Nope. We're not in danger now," she said, and if the words hadn't stuck in her throat, she'd have added, "but Frisbee is."

"Let's look at Frisbee now, before the other patients start arriving," said Dr. Emily as if she'd read Mandy's mind. "It shouldn't take long." She led the way into her examining room. Amber hopped behind her on one leg, leaning on James's arm.

There was hardly a sound in the room while Dr. Emily checked Frisbee's eye. She studied the pink lump and pulled down Frisbee's lower eyelid for a closer look. Then she straightened up and said to Dr. Adam, "What do you think?"

Dr. Adam bent over Frisbee, too. A moment or two later, they exchanged a somber look. Mandy's heart dropped to her boots. She put a hand on Amber's arm, ready to comfort her.

"It's what I thought when I saw Frisbee at the farm," said Dr. Emily. "Glandular hypertrophy."

"Glandular hypertrophy!" Amber gasped. Mandy was briefly impressed that she could even pronounce the condition. "What's that?"

Mandy was in the dark, too. The unfamiliar term sounded as terrible as it looked.

"It's also called cherry eye," Dr. Emily explained. "It's when the gland of the dog's third eyelid prolapses."

"Prolapses?" echoed James, looking puzzled.

"Gives way," Dr. Adam translated. "That's what causes the pink swelling."

Amber was as white as a sheet. "Is it . . . ?" She choked on the words as she fought back tears.

"Is it serious?" said Dr. Emily.

Amber nodded.

"Yes, it is. But it's not life threatening." Dr. Emily smiled and put her hand on Amber's arm. "There's definitely something we can do to help Frisbee."

It was the best thing Mandy had heard in days, better even than the sound of James's voice calling them from outside the cave earlier. She turned to Amber and they hugged each other with relief before scooping up Frisbee between them to hug him, too.

"I'm so dramatic sometimes," said Amber, laughing and crying at once. "I should have told Linda about Frisbee's eye right at the beginning."

"You had no way of knowing," Dr. Emily said kindly. "Sometimes fear makes us do things we normally wouldn't do."

James was standing on the other side of the table, opposite Mandy and Amber. "I think you were really brave, Amber," he said.

The little beagle must have realized that the mood had changed. He looked around at everyone and wagged his white-tipped tail, then gave a cheerful bark.

Amber stroked his head. "What's the treatment for cherry eye?"

"An operation," said Dr. Emily. "There's a new procedure called the imbrication technique. We cut a sort of pocket into the third eyelid then stitch the swollen gland, which is that pink lump, back into place."

Mandy winced. "It sounds complicated."

"Actually, it's a lot simpler than the operations vets used to do for cherry eye," said Dr. Adam. "And it doesn't take nearly as long."

More good news! But Mandy knew better than to celebrate just yet. "Is the operation always successful?"

"Not always," cautioned Dr. Emily. "Sometimes it has to be done again. But we won't know until a couple of days after the operation. We'll operate first thing in the morning. With any luck, Frisbee could be as good as new by the weekend."

"Not *could* be," Mandy corrected her mom. "*Will* be."

"And now that you know what's wrong with Frisbee,

we have to call your parents, Amber," said Dr. Adam. "And get you to the doctor, Mandy. Maybe you can go to the hospital with Amber."

But neither of them wanted to leave Frisbee. "Who'll look after him?" Mandy protested. Through the open door of the treatment room she could see people starting to arrive with their pets. Very soon, both of her parents would be too busy to be able to keep an eye on the puppy.

"I'll take care of him," offered James.

"And handle Blackie at the same time?" Mandy asked doubtfully.

After some more persuading, Dr. Emily gave in and called the local doctor, Dr. Mason, who agreed to come over to examine Amber and Mandy.

"But if he says you need to go to hospital, there'll be no argument from either of you," Dr. Adam warned before picking up the phone to call Mr. and Mrs. Hutton.

Mandy and Amber exchanged glances and nodded reluctantly. "OK, but only if we absolutely *have* to," Mandy said, and sighed.

Dr. Mason confirmed that Amber's ankle was badly sprained, but they didn't need to go to the hospital. He bandaged it firmly and said she'd have to walk on crutches—he'd brought along a pair in the trunk of his car—for a week or two until it had healed. The cut on Mandy's forehead was deep but wouldn't need stitches.

"I can't believe how lucky you are," commented James after Dr. Mason had left. They were in the living room watching a wildlife program on TV. Mandy and Amber were on the sofa with Frisbee tumbling around on their laps, and James was lying on his stomach with Blackie stretched out next to him. He still looked a little pale, as though losing the girls down a pothole had shocked him to the core.

Amber had telephoned Linda Davis at the Little Briar Dog Rescue Center to explain exactly what was wrong with Frisbee, and to say how sorry she was for taking him. Mandy could tell it wasn't an easy call to make— Amber came back looking tearful—but in the end, Linda had understood that she'd only acted out of love for the puppy, and as long as they were both safe, that was all that mattered. Ms. Davis had even said that Amber was welcome to come back to help out at the center, as soon as her ankle was better.

There was a tap at the door and Jean, the receptionist, came in. "Visitors," she announced, and stepped aside to let them through.

"Amber!" cried an auburn-haired woman. She ran over to the sofa and flung her arms around the girl.

Whatever else she wanted to say was lost as she buried her face in Amber's hair.

An exhausted-looking man followed her and knelt down in front of Amber, taking her hands in his. "We thought we'd lost you," he said, his voice breaking.

Amber's face crumpled and she started to cry. "Mom. Dad." The girl sobbed. She'd been so brave all through the pothole adventure and being rescued, but now she cried and cried. When her dad folded his arms around her and said, "It's OK now. The most important thing is that you're safe," she started crying again — enormous sobs that made her entire body heave.

Mandy and James exchanged a glance that showed they both felt rather awkward at witnessing the reunion, but the Hopes' living room was very small and they couldn't squeeze around Amber and her parents to make their escape. They sat in silence, trying to watch the television screen and not look as if they were intruding.

Frisbee was sitting on Mandy's lap. He must have thought he was missing out on something because he scampered across to Amber, then stood up in her lap and licked her cheek.

"The little cutie!" said Mrs. Hutton, including him in her embrace.

Mandy felt a lump in her throat. She looked away,

meeting James's eyes. She thought she saw him swallow, too.

When Amber was able to speak without bursting into tears, she told her parents everything that had happened from the time she'd run off with Frisbee until the moment James returned with the rescue team. "If it weren't for Mandy and James, and Blackie, of course," she added when he looked up at her and thumped his tail, "I don't know what would have happened to me and Frisbee."

"Maybe you'd have given up and gone home," Mandy told her. She felt a pang of guilt, thinking it was probably her fault that Amber had fallen into the pothole. If Mandy hadn't come up with the idea of searching for her, they wouldn't have startled her in the ruined barn and Amber wouldn't have run off blindly across the moor.

"Never," Amber said softly. "I was too worried about Frisbee. I'd have stayed away forever if you hadn't found me."

Mr. Hutton squeezed onto the sofa next to Amber. He put his arm around her shoulder and held her so close it looked as if he would never let her go again. He smiled at Mandy and James. "We're so grateful for your help."

James looked embarrassed. "It was nothing," he said, hiding his scarlet cheeks by bending over to pet Blackie.

Mandy shrugged and said modestly, "It wasn't such a

big deal." And as far as she was concerned, it wasn't. She'd have gone to the ends of the earth to help anyone — person or animal — in distress. And in this case, there was an added bonus. She'd made a new friend.

Mr. Hutton stood up and took his car keys out of his pocket. "I think it's time we went home. Ready, Amber?" He offered her his hand to help her get up.

Amber's face dropped. She looked at Frisbee, then up at her dad, then back to Frisbee again. "I . . . er . . ."

Mandy guessed that Amber couldn't bear to be parted from the puppy, especially on the eve of his big operation. She would have felt exactly the same in Amber's place. "What about letting her stay with us for a few days?" she suggested. "At least until Frisbee's recovered from his operation."

"That's kind of you, but we couldn't," said Mrs. Hutton. She stood up and got the crutches that were leaning against the wall. "Amber's going to need lots of help."

"That's no problem," Mandy said. "I'll take care of her." Amber shot her a grateful look.

"Mandy's a great nurse," said James. "She's nursed just about every type of living thing you can think of, from dogs and cats to giraffes and gorillas. A human with a sprained ankle will be easy compared to some of her patients."

Mandy grinned at him. "And you're a pretty good partner," she said. There were very few times when he hadn't been right alongside her, caring for an injured or sick animal.

Mr. and Mrs. Hutton looked at each other. "I'm not sure," said Mrs. Hutton hesitantly. "What do you think, Len?"

Her husband rubbed his hand over his face and looked at Amber.

Mandy quickly left to find Dr. Emily, and confirm that Amber was welcome at their home for a few days. She was sure her mother's approval would help Amber's case with her own parents.

"See! It's all right with everyone," Amber pleaded upon Mandy's return. "I'll be fine, I promise!" When her mom and dad still didn't say anything, she added, "I won't run away again." She fondled Frisbee's silky ears. "I don't have to now."

Her words seemed to reassure her mom and dad and they finally agreed to let her stay at Animal Ark for a few more days. "Just until that pup's out of the woods," said Mrs. Hutton, and Amber's face lit up so much that Mandy winced. However hard her parents tried, there was still no guarantee that the operation on Frisbee's eye would be a success.

Immediately after breakfast the next morning, Mandy and Amber went to see Frisbee in the residential unit.

"I see that not even sprained ankles and cut foreheads can keep you two away from that little dog," said a smiling Dr. Adam as they went out of the kitchen, Amber swinging herself along on the crutches and Mandy going ahead to open the door.

"*Nothing* could keep us away from him," Mandy remarked. It was true that her forehead was hurting — the pain had woken her up several times in the night. So, too, had a nightmare in which a wall of water had rushed through the tunnel, taking her and Amber and Frisbee with it. *The worst never happened*, she had to keep reminding herself as she lay in bed with the terrifying image playing over and over in her mind.

Frisbee was delighted to see them. He stood up against the wire mesh of his comfortable cage and sniffed at their hands, hoping for a treat.

"Sorry," Mandy told him. She opened the gate and took him out. "You can't eat until after your operation."

"And then you'll probably be feeling too groggy to want anything," said Amber, smoothing the top of his head. She was supporting herself on one crutch and had propped the other one against the wall so that she had a free hand.

Frisbee gazed up at his two adoring fans. The ugly pink swelling in his eye must have been very uncomfortable,

but he wagged his tail happily before licking Amber's hand.

The door to the unit opened and Simon came in. "We're ready for him," he announced. He came over and took Frisbee from Mandy.

"This is it," Amber said, patting Frisbee once more. She cast an anxious look at Simon. "You'll be careful with him, won't you?"

"More careful than you can imagine," Simon promised. "Dr. Emily's a wonderful surgeon."

After Simon and Frisbee had left, it felt very empty in the residential unit. There was only one other patient, a young male cat who was to be neutered later that morning. Mandy and Amber spent a few minutes visiting him, then Mandy suggested they go to see Portia. The magnificent bird might help take Amber's mind off Frisbee.

"She's really stunning, but Mom and Dad haven't been able to figure out what's wrong with her," Mandy said, pushing open the door of the wildlife unit. "So she's not looking her best right now."

This was an understatement. Portia looked worse than ever. "She's gone downhill so much!" Mandy gasped.

Portia huddled at the end of her perch, her head hanging over her keel. Her bones jutted out underneath her dull, unkempt feathers, and she didn't even bother to look at them, not even when Mandy risked putting her finger into the cage to get her attention.

Mandy swallowed hard. "Birds don't show that they're sick until . . ." Her voice faded away. She didn't want to upset Amber by letting her know that this was probably one of those times when there was nothing a vet could do. Being gloomy wouldn't help anyone, least of all Amber, who was worried enough about Frisbee. "I'll clean out her cage and give her some fresh food and water," she said.

Amber leaned against the wall and watched Mandy pull out the bottom of the cage to clean off the macaw's droppings. "What's the matter?" Amber asked when Mandy suddenly stopped and stared down at the tray in her hands.

"I'm not sure," Mandy said. "But I have a feeling this could be important." She pointed to some seeds among the droppings. "See those?"

Amber nodded. "What about them?"

"They haven't been digested," Mandy said. She headed for the door. "My dad should probably see these. Are you coming?"

With Amber swinging along behind her on her crutches, Mandy hurried to her dad's examining room. Before they got there, they met James in the reception area. "Hi, James," Mandy said without stopping.

James started to explain why he'd come to Animal Ark so early. "I couldn't sit around at home waiting for you to call," he began, then gave up. "What's up?" he asked, following them across the waiting room.

Mandy didn't reply. She was already knocking on the exam room door. She pushed it open a crack. "Dad?"

Dr. Adam looked up from his desk. He was filling in a patient's card. "Mmm?" he murmured, then he noticed the tray Mandy was holding. "What's the problem?"

"Look at this." Mandy went over to him and pointed

to the undigested seeds. "I found these in Portia's cage. I know it means something when an animal or a bird doesn't digest food on its way through the stomach."

A light seemed to come on in Dr. Adam's eyes. "Undigested seeds!" He stood up and pulled a book down from a shelf. Mandy, James, and Amber crowded around.

Dr. Adam leafed through the book until he found the section he was looking for. "Here's the answer," he said, stabbing his finger at the page. "It was staring us in the face all along!"

Nine

Mandy looked over his shoulder, her heart beating loudly. "Macaw wasting disease," she read aloud. "What does it mean?"

Dr. Adam looked grave. "It's a very serious virus that attacks the nervous system, particularly the nerves in the crop and stomach, so that the bird can't digest food."

Mandy gasped. "You mean Portia's starving to death?"

"I'm afraid so," Dr. Adam said somberly.

"There must be some sort of treatment," James

insisted. His eyes skimmed over the page. Suddenly, he stopped and frowned.

"What is it?" Mandy asked him, feeling a knot in the pit of her stomach.

James shook his head. "It says here that there's no treatment for the disease," he said quietly.

Mandy bit her lip, hot tears welling behind her eyes.

"Actually, that textbook's a little out of date," said Dr. Adam. "At the time it was published, macaws didn't stand a chance if they contracted the virus. But just recently . . ."

Mandy held her breath.

". . . a new drug has become available."

"You mean you can treat Portia?" Mandy burst out.

"Yes," said Dr. Adam. "As I was trying to say before I was rudely interrupted"—he winked at James and Amber, then smiled at Mandy—"a new anti-inflammatory pill has been developed. It won't cure Portia, but it will keep the virus at bay as long as she takes it twice a day for the rest of her life."

Mandy was so relieved that she only vaguely heard her dad explaining that the tablet had to be crushed up and when Portia would start to improve. But when he said that there may be other macaws with the same illness, she was all ears.

"The disease is transmitted from bird to bird in very

close quarters. So Mr. Parker Smythe was wrong in thinking it might have been something in Welford that didn't agree with Portia," explained Dr. Adam.

"If Portia hasn't been in contact with any other birds since she came to live with him, she must have picked it up in the place she came from," guessed Amber.

"Probably," Dr. Adam agreed.

Amber looked thoughtful. "Where did Portia come from?"

"Mr. Parker Smythe said a friend gave her to him, but she might have been from a breeder or from a pet shop originally," answered Dr. Adam. He put down the book on avian diseases and started to flick through the pages of the telephone directory.

"Perhaps from people who don't know how to prevent macaw wasting disease," suggested Amber. She adjusted her grip on one of the crutches as if it was a bit uncomfortable. Seeing this, James pulled out a chair and Amber gratefully sat down.

"I've heard about people importing exotic birds illegally," Mandy said. "Maybe Portia came from someone like that."

"I've heard about that, too," said Amber. "People can make a lot of money bringing rare birds to this country and selling them to people who don't know how to care for them."

"That's terrible!" Mandy said angrily. "The people selling them probably don't care how the birds are treated, as long as they get paid."

"People like that don't deserve to have anything to do with animals," said Amber, her eyes flashing. "It's as bad as abandoning a litter of beagle puppies."

"We'll have to put a stop to it," Mandy declared.

James hadn't managed to get a word in. He'd watched the girls batting the topic between them, his eyes going from one to the other as if he were watching a tennis match. He looked dizzy when he finally managed to have his say. "Put a stop to what? Importing macaws or abandoning puppies?"

"Both," Mandy said firmly. "But we'll start with the macaw problem. Other macaws from Portia's breeder could be coming down with the wasting disease at this very moment."

"Hold your horses, you two!" Dr. Adam cautioned them. "We can't be sure of that."

But neither Mandy nor Amber listened to him. They resumed their verbal tennis match.

"How do we deal with it?" Amber grabbed her crutches and stood up as if ready to hop all the way to the first breeder.

"First, we have to find out who the breeder is," Mandy

said. She noticed Dr. Adam picking up the phone. "Who are you calling, Dad?"

"The veterinary drug supplier in Walton, to order Portia's medication. We should be able to pick it up this afternoon."

Mandy waited for him to finish placing the order. When he hung up, she said, "You have another call to make."

"Right," her dad said, nodding. "To the Parker Smythes' to tell them about Portia."

"And to ask them for the breeder's address and phone number," Mandy added.

"So we can tell the breeder about Portia's condition, that's all," said Mandy's dad, and he looked at her sternly. "And not to imply that there's any funny business going on. Because we have no proof of that, right?"

"All right," Mandy said. But she had already convinced herself that the breeder was up to no good.

Mr. Parker Smythe was relieved and grateful to hear that Portia's illness had at last been diagnosed. He didn't know who the breeder was but gave Dr. Adam the phone number of Adrian Birch, the colleague who had bought Portia for him.

"You can call Adrian Birch, if you like," Dr. Adam told Mandy after he'd finished talking to Mr. Parker Smythe.

He passed her the piece of paper on which he'd jotted down the number. "But please don't imply that he bought Portia from a shady dealer!"

Mandy dialed the number and waited breathlessly. Whatever her dad said, could they be on the trail of an illegal bird trader? "Mr. Birch?" she said when a man answered. She introduced herself before filling him in about Portia.

Mr. Birch seemed very upset by the news. "But she's magnificent," he said. "She showed no sign of any illness when I bought her, and Tessa Kramer's the most reputable of all the local breeders. I've known her for several years. I bought my two hyacinth macaws, Caliban and Miranda, from her, and they've never been sick a day."

Mandy began to think she might have been wrong about the breeder. It sounded as if Adrian Birch had a lot of confidence in her, which couldn't mean she was importing exotic birds illegally and in poor health. Mandy felt bad about jumping to conclusions — and the look her dad was giving her suggested he could read her mind — but she knew it was important to speak to Tessa Kramer. Her birds could be at risk. "Do you think she'd agree to see us?" she asked Mr. Birch. "I mean, she needs to know about Portia, doesn't she?"

"Absolutely," agreed Mr. Birch, and he gave Mandy Tessa's phone number and address.

"Eight Paradise Valley Road, Walton," Mandy said, writing down the details. She hung up and saw that Simon had come into the room. He was still wearing a green surgery mask, but he'd pushed it down so that it hung below his chin. Was Frisbee's operation over already? Mandy glanced at Amber and saw that she was looking expectantly at Simon.

Amber started to ask about the puppy, but Simon spoke at the same time and appeared not to hear her. "Eight Paradise Valley? Isn't that Tessa Kramer's place?" he asked as he opened a cupboard and took out some instruments.

Mandy nodded. "That's where Portia came from. We need to see her and tell her that Portia's got macaw wasting disease." She was ready to hop onto her bike then and there and cycle the three miles to Walton. It would mean leaving Amber behind because of her sprained ankle, but she probably wouldn't mind that much.

Simon whistled. "Wasting disease! That's bad news."

Amber opened her mouth to speak again, but James beat her to it. "Not so bad now that there's a new drug," he said.

"There is?" asked Simon, looking at Dr. Adam.

"That's right. I've ordered it. Would you mind going to Walton to pick it up for me later?" Dr. Adam replied.

Mandy saw a chance to include Amber. "And you could give us a ride when you go, couldn't you?" she said.

"Yes and yes, to both questions," said Simon, going to the door. "But you'll have to wait for half an hour until we finish with Frisbee."

"How is he?" Amber at last found the opportunity to speak, and Mandy crossed her fingers as she waited for Simon's reply.

"Hard to say," he told them. "He's still being operated on." Simon smiled at them. "But don't worry, I promise you'll be the first to know as soon as I have some news."

It felt like one of the longest half hours of Mandy's life. Amber's, too. "Hard to say," she repeated more than once after the three friends had gone into the residential unit to make sure Frisbee would come back to the most comfortable bed he'd ever slept in. "What did Simon mean by that?"

Mandy wasn't sure. Could it mean that the procedure was more difficult than Dr. Emily had anticipated?

James had a more practical outlook. "It's obviously hard to say if an operation's a success before it's over." But it turned out that his calmness was only on the outside. When Simon pushed open the door twenty minutes later, cradling Frisbee in his arms, James dropped the bowl of water he was carrying with a clatter in his haste to greet the puppy.

Mandy had just swept out the cage, and Amber was

putting a clean blanket inside it. "Is he all right?" they both demanded, hurrying over.

"He's fine," said Simon, and he stood still for a moment so that they could all look at the puppy. "But we'll have to wait a few days before we can give him the all clear."

Frisbee lay sleeping in Simon's arms, his head cradled in the crook of his elbow. Apart from being very groggy, there was no obvious sign that he'd just had an operation.

"Why doesn't he have a bandage over his eyes?" Mandy asked.

"The surgery wasn't invasive," Simon explained. "It was more like doing a little sewing, putting in a stitch to repair the prolapse."

Amber touched the top of Frisbee's head. "Will he be asleep for long?"

"Not too long," said Simon. "We gave him a short-acting general anesthetic." He carried Frisbee to the cage and put him on the soft bed.

The puppy must have felt the change from Simon's warm arms to the fleecy blanket because he opened his eyes and blinked. The affected eye was very swollen, but Mandy forced herself to look closely at it. The ugly pink lump was gone!

Amber had noticed the change, too. "Frisbee!" she whispered, putting a hand against the cage. "You look fantastic."

Even though everything must have looked a bit hazy, Frisbee seemed to recognize them. He whined softly and managed to wag the end of his tail before he closed his eyes again.

Just then, Dr. Emily came in. "I know it looks good. But that's because we've stitched the prolapsed gland behind the third eyelid. Now we have to hope that the knot of the stitch doesn't rub on the cornea and cause an ulcer. I'll keep checking for that, but we'll have to wait until Friday afternoon before we know the final outcome," she cautioned them.

Friday afternoon! That seemed light-years away. It was also the day before Halloween, Mandy suddenly remembered. Her mind started to race. *Ghosts, witches, spells, magic, bad luck* ... She stifled the superstitions that crowded her mind. After all, that's exactly what they were, silly superstitions. Just because it was Halloween didn't mean that you couldn't have some good luck as well.

Fifteen minutes later, thoroughly satisfied that Frisbee was comfortable, Mandy, James, and Amber piled into Simon's rattling old van for the short trip to Walton.

"See you in about half an hour," Simon told them when he dropped them outside 8 Paradise Valley Road.

It was a neat suburban house, and as ordinary as the

others in the road except that the front door was painted a bright blue.

"It's almost the same color as Portia," Mandy pointed out to James and Amber. "Even the number's the color of her eye rings."

There was a large bright yellow number 8 on the door below a brass knocker in the shape of a parrot.

Mandy hesitated before lifting the knocker. She could hear squawks coming from the back of the house, and she wondered just how many exotic birds were kept here. More important, she wondered what their living conditions were like and how well they were being treated. Mr. Birch had sounded confident about Ms. Kramer's experience, but you couldn't escape the fact that Portia was fighting for her life against a savage and highly infectious disease. Finding the courage to face the breeder, Mandy lifted the brass parrot and rapped it against the door.

A few moments later, the door opened to reveal a tiny woman, shorter than Mandy, with long black hair and huge blue eyes. Her fingernails were painted bright crimson and she had gold rings on almost every finger. She was wearing bright yellow gym pants and a rainbow-colored sweater that reminded Mandy of a clown. And on her shoulder, like the cherry on a cake, was a green lovebird that nibbled at her ear and hair.

"Ms. Kramer?" Mandy stammered.

"That's me," said the woman. "May I help you?"

The lovebird on her shoulder stopped nibbling. It looked at the three strangers for a second before uttering an earsplitting squawk that must have practically deafened the woman.

"The thing is . . ." James began.

"We've come to see your macaws," Amber finished for him. "You see, we think they could be in danger." She sounded really confident, like someone who worked for an animal rights organization.

"In danger? From what?" Ms. Kramer looked horrified.

"Macaw wasting disease," Mandy explained. "A hyacinth macaw that came from here has just been diagnosed with it."

Ms. Kramer's jaw dropped open, and the color drained from her cheeks. "That's dreadful news!" She glanced over her shoulder toward the shrill birdcalls in the background.

She's just like a bird herself, Mandy thought, looking at her tiny frame and bright eyes.

Amber was growing bolder by the minute. "There must be a problem with the way the macaws are being kept," she said, but Ms. Kramer didn't seem to hear her. She'd turned away and was hurrying back inside.

Halfway down the hall she stopped and looked back. "Oh, I am sorry," she said. "I'm forgetting my manners. Do come in. I'll make you some tea. But first I need to see to the pretties."

Mandy assumed she meant her birds.

"I must look closely to see if any of them are sick," continued the birdlike woman.

All of Mandy's suspicions about Portia's breeder vanished. Ms. Kramer wasn't a ruthless exploiter of exotic birds but someone who obviously cared a great deal about her pets.

"May we come and see the birds, too?" asked Amber.

"Yes, of course!" Ms. Kramer answered without a moment's hesitation, making Mandy even more certain that she had nothing to hide.

They followed Ms. Kramer along the hall and through a door into a short, enclosed passage that led to another door. This one opened out to what had at one time been a walled garden, but had now been transformed into a spectacular glass-enclosed aviary. Mandy felt as if she'd arrived in a tropical paradise!

Dozens of magnificent macaws and parrots flew around, or sat on branches preening their rainbow feathers or perched to feed from trays filled with all sorts of tropical fruit. They squawked and called loudly. Mandy was tempted to block her ears, but decided not

to. She didn't want to miss any part of this incredible, brightly colored world.

James and Amber looked equally amazed. "It's like finding yourself in the Amazon!" whispered James, his eyes sparkling behind his glasses.

Ms. Kramer smiled at him. "I'm glad you think so. Because that's how I think of this place. My own private jungle." She gave Amber the green lovebird to hold. "Look after Amigo for me, please," she said. "I need to make sure none of the macaws have lost weight." Calling each one by its name, she went from bird to bird and looked closely at them. Some were too high for her to reach. For those, she picked up a piece of fruit and held out her hand. "Come on," she'd say. "Come to Tessa," and to Mandy's astonishment, the macaws took turns descending from their high perches or swooping down with a flap of their powerful wings.

"We'll look for undigested seeds," Mandy offered, and she and James checked for seeds or husks on the floor. They were very relieved when they didn't find any. It would be a tragedy if any of these gorgeous birds got sick like Portia had.

Ms. Kramer seemed very pleased that none of her birds showed any obvious signs of the disease. "But I'll call in a macaw specialist to examine them," she said. "Just in case I've missed something."

Mandy nodded. For once, she didn't recommend her own parents because she knew that although they were great veterinarians, neither her mom nor her dad would claim to be an avian specialist.

Ms. Kramer took them into her living room, which was as colorful as everything else, then disappeared into the kitchen to make tea. Amigo the lovebird was snuggled against the side of her head once more. She returned five minutes later with a teapot shaped like a parrot, a pitcher of juice, and a cake topped with green icing. She poured a cup of tea for herself and juice for her guests and gave them each a slice of cake. Mandy was a bit reluctant to eat it, but James had no trouble with the unlikely color and happily took Mandy's piece when Ms. Kramer wasn't looking.

"Your birds are obviously very well cared for," Mandy ventured. "They couldn't have spread the disease to Portia."

"I sincerely hope they didn't," said Ms. Kramer. She dabbed at her mouth with a napkin. "But about a month ago, I was looking after a macaw that had been illegally imported. The Society for the Protection of Birds had confiscated it from a pet shop, and I offered to care for it until a good home was found. I'm always reluctant to take birds from unknown breeders, but in this case I couldn't resist helping out. Poor Portia must have contracted the disease from her." She shook her head. "Which means the confiscated bird must be suffering, too. The things people do to make money!"

She finished her tea and stood up. "If you'll excuse me, I need to call the new owner of that bird and the macaw specialist."

It was time for Mandy and the others to go. Through the window they caught a glimpse of Simon's van coming along the road. His timing was perfect! "Thank you so much for letting us see your birds," Mandy said.

"On the contrary," said Ms. Kramer. "Thank *you* for coming to see them. And for warning me about this disease." She held Mandy's hands in her own and looked intently at her. "I do hope your parents can help Portia, and that it's not too late for her. Such a beautiful bird doesn't deserve to be sick. Please, give her my love when you see her."

Part of Mandy thought it was one of the strangest requests she'd ever heard, but on the other hand it seemed totally reasonable. Ms. Kramer clearly loved her birds, even the ones that had gone to new owners. "I will," she promised, silently echoing Ms. Kramer's hope.

Ten

"Hold still a minute, Frisbee," Mandy said when she and Amber went to see the puppy the following morning. She was trying to squeeze a dab of cortisone ointment into the corner of his eye. Her mom had explained that the ointment would help reduce the swelling. "That's a good boy," she said when she'd finished.

"He *is* good," said Amber. She was sitting on a chair, holding the puppy in her lap. "And that's exactly what I told my mom and dad." She'd called them last night to give them the latest news about Frisbee.

Even though it was only twenty-four hours since the operation, Frisbee was pretty much his normal, cheerful

124

self again. When Mandy and Amber had come in earlier, he'd stood up against the side of his cage and whined excitedly. And when Mandy took him out and gave him to Amber, he was so pleased to see her he couldn't stop licking her face.

"If he's in any pain, he's certainly not showing it," said Amber. "You're a very brave little dog," she told him.

"Let's see if he's a hungry little dog," Mandy said, bringing him a bowl of food.

When Frisbee saw her coming with the dish, he squirmed and let out a tiny whine.

"He's hungry, all right," Amber said, grinning. She put him on the ground and he jumped up at Mandy until she placed the dish on the floor in front of him.

It took less than a minute for him to scarf down his breakfast. As soon as he'd finished, he looked around greedily for more.

"You're as bad as my dad and James," smiled Mandy. She picked up the bowl to take it to the sink. "Whoever you go to live with will have to be careful not to over-feed you."

At once, a shadow passed across Amber's face, and Mandy kicked herself. There was no need to remind Amber that Frisbee wouldn't stay at the dog rescue center forever.

There was something else on Amber's mind, too. "*If*

he goes to a new home," she said quietly, and Mandy guessed she was worrying about whether the operation would turn out to be a success.

Dr. Emily came in. "I need to take him for an eye test," she explained, picking Frisbee up from Amber's lap.

"Oh, he can see," Amber said confidently. "He recognized us right away, and he could see his food bowl even before Mandy put it on the floor." Mandy suspected that she was trying to convince not only Dr. Emily that Frisbee could see just fine but herself, too.

"It's not his sight that I'm testing," said Dr. Emily. "That shouldn't have been affected at all. I need to check for ulcers on his cornea."

"How do you do that?" Mandy asked, hoping it wouldn't involve another anesthetic.

Dr. Emily tucked Frisbee under her arm and massaged his ears. "I'll put a drop of fluorescent stain in his eye. It's a pale, greeny color. If it sticks to the cornea, the clear outer covering on his eye, it means there's a break. If that's the case, I'll change his ointment. It just means the previous ointment prevented it from healing." Frisbee started nibbling her hands. "Come on, little guy, let's have a look at you," she said, turning to go. She glanced back at Amber who was biting a nail. "It won't hurt him, I promise," Dr. Emily reassured her.

Once her mom had gone, Mandy tried to take Amber's

mind off Frisbee. "We have another patient to see, remember?" She meant Portia. She helped Amber to stand up, then gave her the crutches that had been propped in the corner.

Portia was still the only occupant in the wildlife unit, and she looked a little lonely in there. She'd had her first dose of medicine the night before, and Mandy knew not to expect any improvement so soon. But she was still disappointed when Portia barely even glanced at them. Mandy thought of Ms. Kramer's lively, happy birds who swooped around their miniature Amazon jungle. Portia was so subdued that it was impossible to imagine her being anything like them.

Mandy was changing Portia's drinking water when Simon came in with the next dose of medicine. "I thought I'd find you here," he said. "You can give me a hand with this." He gave the syringe containing the solution of crushed-up pills to Mandy. "I'll hold her for you."

He took Portia out of her cage and tucked her under one arm. Then he opened her beak. "OK, now!" he instructed, and Mandy quickly squirted the medicine into Portia's mouth.

The macaw was so weak she didn't bother to even shake her head. When Simon put her back in her cage, she sat hunched up in a corner, her feathers sticking out in disarray.

Amber was sitting on an upturned crate, watching. "She *will* get better, won't she?" she asked with a frown.

Simon nodded. "Dr. Adam has a lot of confidence in this medication."

But looking at Portia fluffed up in her corner, it was hard to believe she'd recover.

Mrs. Parker Smythe was just as dismayed by the sight of Portia when she and her husband arrived to visit the bird later. "Oh, my! She does look weak," she said, gasping. "She's even worse than when she first came in."

Mr. Parker Smythe's reaction was more positive. "Yes, but at least we know she's going to survive, thanks to Adam's treatment. I don't mind if we have to dose her for the rest of her life, as long as it makes her feel better. In a few weeks, she'll be as magnificent as before."

"I hope so," said his wife. "It would be a shame to have new birds that don't compliment the dining room colors as beautifully."

Mandy and Amber exchanged a look of horror. You couldn't treat a bird as an accessory to a room! As if she agreed, Portia let out a raucous squawk.

Mandy felt a burst of hope. It was the first sound the macaw had made in days.

"That's my girl!" said Mr. Parker Smythe, his face

lighting up. "You *must* be feeling better if you can shout like that."

A few minutes after the Parker Smythes had left, there was more encouraging news. Dr. Emily popped her head around the door to the wildlife unit. "Just thought you'd like to know that I can't see any problems in Frisbee's eye!" she reported.

Mandy and Amber hugged each other with relief.

"But I'll need to do one more test on Friday to make sure all is well," Dr. Emily reminded them.

"So far, so good," said Amber with a nervous smile.

A little before five o'clock on Friday afternoon, Mandy, James, and Amber were in the residential unit with Frisbee. Dr. Emily had only one more patient to see before she could perform the final test on Frisbee — to make sure that there were definitely no problems and that the stitches were in the right place.

Amber was so nervous she could hardly keep still. "What if the stitches aren't in right?" she asked for the twentieth time.

"Then Mom will have to operate again," Mandy told her patiently.

They were sitting on a large mat on the floor of the unit. Frisbee was in the middle, playing with a selection of toys—a rubber ball, a piece of rope, an old slipper. He picked up the rope and offered it to Amber, inviting her to play tug-of-war.

"Not bad for someone who's just had an operation," smiled James. "He's going to grow up to be a great dog. His new owner is going to be very lucky."

"That's going to be me!" Amber's statement was so unexpected, Mandy thought she hadn't heard correctly.

"You said it *is* or *isn't* going to be you?" she checked.

"It *is* going to be me," answered Amber, sounding very determined. Her eyes shone. "I'm going to ask Linda and my parents if I can keep Frisbee."

Mandy bit her lip. Amber could be setting herself up for a big disappointment if her parents didn't agree. "That would be fantastic," she said slowly.

"Yeah," agreed James. "You'd be the best owner Frisbee could have."

"But—" Mandy paused and took a deep breath. "What if your parents won't let you keep him?"

Amber looked downcast. "What you really mean is that I won't be allowed to keep him because I ran away."

"Er . . . no . . ." Mandy said. But to be honest, the thought had crossed her mind. "Puppies are a lot of work, and your mom and dad might not want that kind of responsibility," she added quickly, trying to make up for letting Amber think she didn't trust her. "My parents won't let me have a pet of my own because they say we have enough animals to care for as it is."

"Well, it's different for me," Amber objected. "There isn't a single animal in our house. No one can take care of Frisbee as well as I can. We've bonded and he'll be miserable if I can't keep him. They'll have to listen to me."

Mandy saw there was no point in arguing with her. She just hoped that Amber wouldn't have her heart broken when her parents came to pick her up that evening.

Simon stuck his head around the door. "Dr. Emily's ready for Frisbee now."

"OK. We'll bring him in," Mandy said. She picked up the puppy, and James helped Amber to her feet.

"You have lots of supporters, Frisbee," a smiling Dr. Emily said as they trooped into the examining room. Then, more seriously, she said, "Frisbee needs to be very still when I'm examining him. Perhaps you three should wait outside."

Mandy knew her mom was right. "See you later, Frisbee!" she said, patting his head.

"Good luck, sweetie," said Amber, and she gave him one last cuddle before following Mandy and James out of the room.

A tense wait followed. It was broken briefly when Mr. and Mrs. Hutton arrived, early.

"Mom! Dad!" exclaimed Amber. "I wasn't expecting you yet!"

"I know, but we couldn't wait any longer to take you home," Mrs. Hutton admitted with a warm smile. She looked much better than the last time Mandy had seen her, when her face had been pale and there had been dark circles under her eyes.

"Well, I'm not ready yet. We're still waiting for Frisbee." Amber explained about the final eye examination.

Amber's dad sat down next to her. "I suppose the welcome-home dinner can wait a bit longer," he joked, squeezing her hand.

At last, Dr. Emily emerged with Frisbee in her arms. Mandy tried to read the expression on her mom's face, but Dr. Emily wasn't giving anything away. "The swelling's down so I was able to have a really good look at him," she began. "The fluorescein didn't stick to the cornea so there is no ulceration, and the stitches don't lie directly over the prolapsing gland. It's in the conjunctival fornix."

Mandy couldn't stand it any longer. The technical

words were baffling enough to her, but to Amber's mom and dad, it must have sounded like a different language! "Is he OK?" she blurted out.

"That's what I'm getting to," said Dr. Emily, and Mandy thought there was a glimmer of a smile at the corners of her mouth. "There are no breaks and the stitches are exactly where they should be. The operation was a complete success!"

"Oh!" Mandy took Frisbee from her mom and hugged him quickly before handing him to Amber.

Amber couldn't take him because she was crying too hard. And then she began to laugh. "I can't believe he's going to be OK." She gulped, bursting into tears again.

"What's important is that you're *both* going to be OK," her mom said quietly.

"Yes. You've had a pretty rough time," Dr. Emily agreed.

As if Amber needed reminding, James listed all she'd been through. "Sleeping out in freezing temperatures, running across the moor, falling into a pothole, spraining your ankle, nearly drowning . . ."

Amber wiped her eyes. "I don't care. As long as Frisbee's all right! But I know I shouldn't have run away." She reached up and took the puppy from Mandy.

"I'm glad to hear that," said her dad. "Because that's the one condition we're laying down."

"One condition?" frowned Amber.

Mandy caught her breath. She looked at James, who had his fingers crossed on the seat beside him.

"One condition," Mr. Hutton repeated. "As long as you promise to never do anything as wild as running away again, then we can speak with Linda about Frisbee coming home with us. For good."

Amber looked as if she could hardly believe her ears. Even though she'd been determined to ask her mom and dad if she could keep Frisbee, Mandy could tell that she'd been afraid they'd say no after everything that had happened. "I promise!" she practically yelled. "Thank you! Thank you, Mom and Dad!" She swallowed, fighting back more tears of joy. "Did you hear that, Frisbee? You're coming to live with us!"

After long good-byes, the Huttons had left for the Little Briar Center, taking a happy Frisbee with them. Animal Ark seemed very quiet. Mandy and James cleaned out Frisbee's cage and went to check on Portia. She would be going home only when she started to improve.

The bird blinked at them in recognition and then lowered her head to peck at a piece of mango that Mandy had given her earlier.

"You know, I think she's really enjoying that," Mandy remarked quietly to James without taking her eyes off the bird. When Portia didn't regurgitate the fruit, but sat on her perch looking very comfortable, she was sure the macaw had finally turned the corner. It was like someone had just lifted a huge backpack stuffed with several *dozen* beagle puppies off of Mandy's shoulders.

"You're going to be all right!" she announced jubilantly. She offered Portia another piece of mango. The bird hopped down from her perch and took the fruit, then looked at Mandy and let out a loud squawk.

James chuckled. "I think she's saying thank you."

Mandy and James stayed with Portia a while longer. Just as they were leaving, there was a knock at the door.

"I wonder who that is," said James. He opened the door that led to the residential unit and the rest of the clinic. No one was there.

Mandy burst out laughing. "You've been tricked! It was Portia!" She glanced back at the macaw. "Great trick, Portia."

Portia's little joke jolted Mandy and James into remembering that they'd done nothing about Halloween.

"It's a little late now to start making costumes and thinking up practical jokes," said James when they were having a snack in the kitchen.

"Can't you just wear a white sheet and make scary noises? That should scare people half to death!" teased Dr. Adam.

Mandy joked back. "Especially if you come with us, Dad." Then she grew serious. "Let's forget about tricks and do something different this year."

"Like what?" asked James.

"Like this," Mandy said, and she told him her idea.

The sun had long since set and the stars were starting to come out when Mandy and James met Amber outside the Fox and Goose on Halloween night.

"So, you didn't have any trouble getting your mom and dad to drive you over?" Mandy asked Amber. After working out the smaller details of her Halloween plan with James the night before, she'd called Amber to invite her to join them.

"They think it's a great idea," said Amber. "And Frisbee agrees. It seems like a good way to make it up to Linda, after all the trouble I caused." She turned around to show Mandy that she was wearing her backpack.

"I bet I know what's in there," said James, chuckling. A moment later, a familiar little brown-and-white face peeped out—a face with a quickly healing eye.

"Hi there, little pocket beagle!" Mandy leaned forward to give the puppy a kiss on the top of his head.

But Frisbee beat her to it and gave her a joyous slurping lick right across her face.

"Can you help me take the backpack off?" said Amber. "Everything's in there with Frisbee."

Mandy took Frisbee out, and James eased the pack off Amber's shoulders.

"OK. Here's what I brought," said Amber. She reached into the backpack and brought out a tin can. There was a white label on it with large black lettering that spelled out LITTLE BRIAR DOG RESCUE CENTER.

"Perfect," Mandy said.

Next, Amber took out a stack of flyers. "Linda gave me these to hand out, too. They're full of information about the center and the great work they do with lost and abandoned dogs."

James rolled his eyes. "Don't get me wrong—I love animals as much as you guys do. But it does feel like someone's cloned Mandy!"

The girls shot him a look and he laughed. "Let's get going," he said, taking the tin from Amber, and picking up a large box.

"Is that the candy?" asked Amber.

"Uh-huh. Merry's chocolates, including my very own Jolly Jims," James declared.

"It's a miracle there are any left," Mandy teased. "Or should I say, it's thanks to Amber and Frisbee that James hasn't eaten them all. He just didn't have the time."

"That's a lie!" retorted James. "I knew we'd need them for tonight, so I didn't eat any on purpose."

"Oh, yeah. Like pigs might fly on purpose," Mandy joked.

The three friends set off on the route around the village that Mandy and James had planned. Frisbee peered out from the backpack, which Mandy wore on her front. Next to her, Amber expertly propelled herself forward on her crutches while James was on her other side, carrying the giant box of chocolates and the collection tin. They couldn't have looked less like a group of Halloween tricksters if they'd tried.

Their first stop was the row of tiny cottages that ran down the side of the Fox and Goose. Mandy knocked on the door of the first cottage where Walter Pickard lived.

Mr. Pickard opened the door and held out a basket of candies. "No tricks tonight, please," he said with a smile. "Have a treat." He was a big man with a gentle, friendly voice.

"No. *You* have a treat," said James, offering him one of the chocolates and holding out the tin.

"In exchange for a donation to rescued dogs," Amber explained, presenting one of the flyers.

"Little Briar Dog Rescue Center?" Walter read out loud.

"It's where this little guy came from," Mandy said, and she opened the backpack with a flourish.

Frisbee popped his head out and looked around, his eyes as bright as the stars above.

"What a handsome little pup," said Walter. "Little Briar must be a good place. I'll make a donation." He dug into his pockets and brought out a few coins and put them into the can. "Now, let me see," he said, eyeing the chocolates James was offering him. "Which one should I have?"

"Try one of these," suggested James, and proudly pointed to a Jolly Jim.

"You're the expert." Walter smiled as he helped himself to a chocolate.

For the next hour, the three friends made their way through the village, surprising people with their treat-for-donation version of Halloween. No one could resist the tempting chocolates James offered them, but even more irresistible was Frisbee. His appealing expression persuaded many people to dig deep into their pockets.

Eventually, the full collection can was almost too awkward for James to carry, and the box of chocolates was as light as a feather.

"I think we'll go back now," Mandy said. The plan was to return to the Fox and Goose where Amber's parents had gone for a meal. "We must have seen just about everyone in the village."

The Parker Smythes were coming out from the restaurant when Mandy and the others arrived.

"What's this? A holdup?" asked Mr. Parker Smythe when James thrust the collection can at him.

"Not quite," said Mandy, laughing. "But don't be surprised if this little guy steals your heart." She opened the backpack so that Frisbee could show his winning face.

"What a cute little puppy!" enthused Mrs. Parker Smythe. She folded her gloved hands around his face. "Wouldn't you look just too darling in my conservatory?"

Mr. Parker Smythe rolled his eyes. "But not nearly as magnificent as Portia looks in the dining room," he said. Mandy grinned at James. It sounded as if Mr. Parker Smythe didn't want any more pets used as interior decor! He opened his wallet, peeled out several bills, and pushed them through the slit in the can.

James opened the box of chocolates. "Oops!" he said in a small voice. "They're all gone."

"No, there were two left!" Mandy said. "You ate them, James!"

He shrugged. "I thought we ran out of people to ask for donations."

Mr. Parker Smythe wasn't at all upset about being cheated out of his treat. "Never mind," he said. "I've already had my treat."

"What's that?" Mandy asked.

"Knowing that Portia's getting better and that she'll be home soon, keeping us amused again," said Mr. Parker Smythe. "You know, I've really missed having her around. Imogen even caught me talking to thin air the other day when I forgot Portia wasn't in her cage."

So she wasn't simply a decoration in the Parker Smythe household but a much-loved animal companion. Mandy beamed with delight. "She's got a sense of humor," she agreed. "She had James answering doors last night."

"That sounds like Portia," said Mr. Parker Smythe. "Good at playing tricks. But gorgeous as well."

Just then Frisbee wriggled wildly inside the backpack. "OK, OK!" said Mandy. She lifted him out and held him in her arms. He looked around with his ears pricked — or as pricked as his heavy, floppy ears ever could be. "You're gorgeous, too." And as they headed over to meet Amber's parents, the can full of donations making a very satisfying clinking sound, Mandy thought what an unusual Halloween week it had been.

There had been tension, tears, and danger in big doses, but in the end everything had turned out a treat.